PepperTide

JACK WEYLAND

Deseret Book Company
Salt Lake City, Utah

©1983 Deseret Book Company
All rights reserved
Printed in the United States of America
First printing February 1983

Library of Congress Cataloging in Publication Data

Weyland, Jack, 1940-
   PepperTide.
   I. Title.
PS3573.E99P4   1983   813'.54   82-25171
ISBN 0-87747-967-4

PepperTide

CHAPTER ONE

When I was fourteen years old, my father announced he had a deal going that would make us all rich. He always had deals on the fire, and it seemed we were always just about to get rich. This one required him to go to Mexico for a few days. He gave me fifty dollars for groceries, put me in charge of my younger brother and sister, threw a sleeping bag in his old pickup, hugged the three of us, and drove away.

That was eleven years ago. It was the last we heard from him until six months ago.

"I have a person-to-person collect call for Jimmy Pepper from Hank Pepper. Will you accept the call?" the operator asked.

"You must have the wrong number," I said.

"Jimmy? It's me—Dad. I saw you on Johnny Carson last week. You were so funny—I died laughing."

"Will you accept the call?" the operator broke in.

"What?" I mumbled, feeling stunned. ". . . I guess so."

". . . Like I said, you were so funny. Even my barber said so."

"Who is this again?"

"It's Dad."

"Where are you?"

"Buffalo, Wyoming. I work at a carwash."

A long silence. "Why did you call?"

"Just to say hello."

"Oh sure. Well, nice hearing from you . . . call again sometime."

"Wait. The reason I never came back . . . I was in jail in Mexico. When I got out, I didn't know how to contact you . . . not till I saw you on TV last week."

"Do you need money, is that why you called?"

He said he didn't need any money.

"Ryan's dead," I said.

There was a long silence. Finally he said, "I heard about it. It was too bad. He was a good boy."

"How do you know what he was? You weren't around to find out."

A long silence. "Can you and Jill come see me?"

I wiped my forehead. "Hank, I'm having a hard time with this. Give me your number and I'll get back to you."

"Who was that?" my wife asked after I'd hung up.

I stared at the phone, worried it might strike again. "My father—he's alive. He wants Jill and me to go see him."

"Are you going?"

"I don't know." I left the house for a walk, trying to fight the flood of memories. Somewhere in my mind a dam had broken, unable to take the strain any longer.

There were three kids in our family. I have a sister, Jill, sixteen months younger, and a brother, Ryan, three years younger.

When Dad left, we were living in a small rental house in Cheyenne. The front door opened into the alley, the only house in town that did. The address was 319½ Holcomb. As a boy, I remember resenting the ½, as if it meant we weren't good enough to merit a whole number. Once I tore it down from where it was tacked on a tree in front of the house, but Jill told on me and I had to put it back.

Both our parents were originally from Utah, but after they were married they never returned. Hank had little use for religion or relatives, both of which were in too plentiful supply in Utah.

There's been a parade of mothers and foster mothers running through our lives. Our real mother died when I was eleven, a victim of a hit-and-run accident along a gravel road near Cheyenne.

Our second mother was a woman Dad met in a truck-stop cafe when he was driving truck. It was less than a year after Mom died. Her name was Joan. We woke up one morning to find a woman rattling around in the kitchen, complaining about the mess. Dad walked in, tucking in his shirt and carrying his shoes and socks, and more or less off-handedly announced, "Oh, this is your new mother."

"We don't want a new mother," I said.

He shrugged his shoulders and sat down to put on his shoes. "Don't matter what you want. You got one, and you better obey her if you know what's good for you."

She made good hash browns and liked to watch TV, but more than anything I remember she looked on the grumpy side of life. If you said it was a nice day, she'd tell you it was going to rain.

We didn't get along very well with her. It wouldn't have been too bad if Dad had been around to smooth things over, but he was still driving for a moving van company. He drove all over the country. We loved it because each time he returned, he'd bring gifts from wherever he'd been. Once he went all the way to Maine and brought back a lobster frozen in ice. We loved to hear him talk about the places he'd been.

I'm not sure exactly what went wrong between him and Joan, or whether they were actually even married. About a year after she'd been there, a man started to drop by and pick her up at nights while Hank was away. She always said she was going to a movie, but there were only two movie theatres in town, and they changed movies once every two weeks, but she was gone four times a week.

When Dad got back from a long trip, they got into an

argument that lasted late into the night. I tried to stay awake to listen, but finally fell asleep.

The next morning she was gone.

"Where's Joan?" Ryan asked.

"Gone," was all Dad ever said about it.

For a while he quit driving so he could watch us. He got a job as a dispatcher for the company. Either it didn't pay much or he didn't like sitting at a desk, because by the time I was fourteen he'd quit.

After that we didn't know what he was doing. He'd be gone for a few days, then suddenly appear with lots of money. It was great when he came back, because he'd take us out for pizza and buy us things. Once he bought us new bicycles, and another time, fishing and camping gear. He'd stay home a week or two and then be gone again. At first he paid a lady to come and stay, but I told him he might as well save his money, that I could cook as well as that lady, who always made casseroles with noodles and cream of mushroom soup. It was years later when I finally realized why most women would rather fix casseroles than just about anything.

That's why he left us alone on that last trip.

We got along okay at first, but after three weeks, with him already two weeks late, I started to wonder.

One day we were playing in an old junk car that perpetually sat in our front yard, which, because the house faced the alley, was everyone else's backyard. To us, the car was a wonderful toy, rich with the smell of mildew and rotting orange peels and grease. In that car we had chased and been chased by outlaws. Sometimes it was even a plane or a rocket.

Ryan was sitting on top of the car eating a peanut butter sandwich while Jill and I played "Famous Actress." It wasn't that much fun for me, but she liked it. She was a famous rich actress, and I was her chauffeur. She'd spend hours rummaging in an old trunk in the basement, where Dad had put Mom's clothes. Then she'd come outside, her face smeared with makeup. She'd get in and order me to take her to the Empire State Building.

While we were playing, I looked back and saw a neighbor lady from across the alley standing at her fence and staring at us long and hard. She'd come to empty her garbage but had already done that. She just stared at us. Then without a word she shook her head and left.

The next day after school a woman came. She said her name was Miss McCormack and that she was a caseworker from the county. For a while I thought she meant she worked in a canning factory. But that isn't what she meant at all.

I couldn't figure why she came, because all she did was sit and look. We were watching TV and having our usual peanut butter sandwiches and milk. She sat on the couch in front of the TV, but didn't seem very interested in the show.

"I can change the channel if you want," I said.

"No, that isn't necessary. Is that your supper?"

Seeing she was a woman, I figured she wouldn't be happy about that being our supper. "In a few minutes," I said, "I'm going in the kitchen and make a nice casserole."

"May I see the kitchen?" she asked.

Before I could say no, she was in there opening cupboards, writing things down on her clipboard.

We had plenty of peanut butter. Once while Hank was working as a dispatcher, he heard about a wrecked semitrailer load of peanut butter. He bought several cases at a good price. Due to various disasters in the trucking industry, our basement was usually full of good deals.

"Do you get paid to do this?" I asked, watching her open the refrigerator and write something down.

"Where's your mother?"

"In heaven," Ryan said proudly.

She wrote on her clipboard.

"We have a stepmother though, and she'll be back any day," I said.

"Where is she?"

"She went away with a man," Ryan said.

Miss McCormack started to write that.

"She didn't either," I interrupted. "She went to visit her sick aunt, but she'll be back any day now."

"How do you know?" Miss McCormack asked.

"She died," I said.

"Who died?" she asked, her pencil ready to pounce on my words.

"My stepmother's aunt. That's why our stepmother will be home any day now. She has no reason to stay there. Tomorrow—she'll be back tomorrow. Won't she, Jillsy?"

I winked at her in our own special code. "Tomorrow," she agreed.

"Then who's that man she always goes to the movies with?" Ryan asked.

"Ryan, go watch TV."

Ryan left.

"And where's your father?" the lady asked.

"Away on business, but he'll be back on Friday. What do you call your job?"

"I'm a social worker."

"What do you write on the paper?"

"My impressions."

"Impressions of what?" Jill asked.

"Of the conditions here," Miss McCormack said.

"We don't have any conditions here," Jill said.

Miss McCormack opened another cupboard—full of peanut butter. There were grocery stores with less peanut butter than we had.

I thought it strange she left before *Gilligan's Island* was even over.

The money Dad left was almost gone. We were down to five dollars. I had a paper route that brought in a few dollars a week.

The next day I was in the kitchen working on an old lawn mower engine Dad had brought home for me once. I liked to take things apart and try to figure out how they worked. I didn't always get them back together, but the engine didn't work anyway, so it wasn't like I was wrecking anything.

Since we ate all our meals around the TV set in the living room, we weren't using the kitchen table for anything. It became my workbench for taking the engine apart.

There was a knock on our back door, which most people thought was our front door, because it was the one that faced the street, or rather faced the house in front of us, which faced the street.

I answered it, thinking it might be the lady with the clipboard again, but it was a guy my age. He asked if my name was Jim Pepper, and I said, "What if it is?" He said his name was Kevin Gallagher. That didn't mean anything to me. He mumbled something about being a president. That made even less sense to me.

"You don't look like any kind of president to me," I said.

"I'm the teachers quorum president."

"I don't want to be no teacher," I grumbled.

"You're supposed to be."

"Who says?"

"God." He was very nervous. He cleared his throat and looked like he was going to either cry or sneeze. "I'm supposed to talk to you. Can I come in?"

I shrugged my shoulders. He followed me inside and sat down on a stool and watched. To tell the truth, I enjoyed making him nervous. I banged the wrenches and grunted a lot like I was a mechanic and knew what I was doing.

He sat there stiff as a board. I noticed he was wearing corduroy slacks.

"Are you a Mormon?" he finally asked.

"Maybe I am," I said, remembering a baptism long

ago at my mother's insistence. I dropped a wrench on the floor. He jumped at the noise.

"You could be in our scout troop."

"Why'd I want to do that?"

"We go camping and fishing."

"I don't care about none of that."

"We learn to do things."

"What kind of things?" I figured I had him, that he'd say something dumb like how great it was to learn to tie knots.

He looked at me for a second, then said, "We learn to fix engines."

"Yeah?" I said, suddenly interested.

"Tomorrow night we're starting a new class on auto mechanics. We have a mechanic in our ward who's going to show us some things. I'll come by and get you."

I'd always figured that if I could ever get that engine working I'd rig it up to my bicycle. But the way I was going, I'd never fix it.

"I might go," I said as negatively as I could.

In a way I figured he was just talk, but he really did come by to pick me up. When we got to the church, he introduced me to Bishop Townsend, who shook my hand and said he was glad I could come.

The bishop introduced me to the scoutmaster. In his uniform, he looked a little like an overweight Jolly Green giant. But once I got to know him, he turned out to be okay—he just happened to like scouting.

There were about 15 other guys in the troop. Not all of them were going to learn about car engines. In fact, Kevin and I were the only ones. I wondered if Kevin hadn't created this whole engine mechanics course on the spot just to get me to go to church with him.

We went to Olson's Garage, and Mr. Olson showed us a lot of things about engines and tools. "When you get a car, make sure you always lock it when you leave, or somebody'll come and steal it. Happens all the time."

"How can they start it without a key?" Kevin asked.

"They hot wire it. So remember to lock up."

The conversation drifted to carburetors.

Afterwards we washed up and went back to church. The bishop asked if I'd had a good time.

"It was okay," I said, trying to sound unimpressed. But when I thought about what I'd have done at home, it was ten times better than that.

The next day we ran out of money. I went out and collected from everyone on my paper route. I found that you can collect from the husbands at night if their wives aren't home, and then collect from the wives the next day. But it wasn't stealing, because I was marking it all down in my book. I just figured it was like paying in advance.

That night we went through our couches and chairs, searching between the frame and springs where money can drop. We found a couple of dollars that way. And we turned in some pop bottles at the store.

The next night I sent Ryan through the neighborhood going door to door, saying he was on a treasure hunt and needed three pop bottles. Jill and I followed with an old wagon to put the bottles in.

I rode my bike to the airport, where there's a fountain where people with nothing better to do throw pennies and nickels and make a wish. I'd made a small rake at home so I could get the money without having to go wading. I got over three dollars that way.

On Saturday morning, while Ryan and Jill watched cartoons, Kevin came and asked us to go to church with him the next day. I didn't really want to go, but he said that after church his parents said it would be all right for us to come to supper. I jumped at the offer.

I don't remember much about the first time in church except in priesthood meeting, Kevin ran the whole show as far as the quorum went. He got up and welcomed everybody and said who'd take care of fixing the sacrament. He told them about me, saying I was a mechanic, and just what their quorum needed for their summer cycling trip.

Mostly I remember the food after church. We ate everything they had, and then, since we were still hungry, Kevin's mother fixed some scrambled eggs. They asked about Dad. I said he'd be back on Wednesday.

Monday after school, Miss McCormack came again, this time with a man. She called him Mr. Ackley. He had on a gray western suit and a bolo tie. I figured he just wore that stuff so people would think he was a regular Westerner—but I could tell he really hated Wyoming. He never spoke directly at us, and when he said anything to her, he talked quietly as if he were telling secrets we weren't supposed to hear.

"Is your father back yet?" Miss McCormack asked.

"Not yet, but he phoned yesterday. He had a little trouble with his truck, but everything's fine now. He's in Omaha now and has to make a delivery in Minnesota. Then he'll be back."

"Hmm," Mr. Ackley said.

We all sat down in the living room. Ryan was watching TV, and Jill was in the basement trying on dresses again and experimenting with eye shadow and rouge.

"We'd like to look around," Miss McCormack said.

"What for?"

"We'd like to evaluate conditions here."

"Is that all you people do?"

Miss McCormack started for the kitchen. Mr. Ackley followed.

They weren't too happy about the jumble of engine parts strewn on the kitchen table. "This is a pigsty," Mr. Ackley said to her.

She opened the refrigerator for him to look in. Green mold was growing on one of Joan's casseroles. He shook his head. "Deplorable," he whispered to Miss McCormack.

Then Jill swirled into the kitchen, unaware of our company. She had eye shadow and rouge all over her face and was wearing one of Joan's old low-cut dresses about four sizes too big. She looked ridiculous. When she saw Mr. Ackley and Miss McCormack, she screamed and ran out again.

"Who was that?" Mr. Ackley whispered.

"The twelve-year-old," Miss McCormack replied.

"Almost thirteen," I added.

"She looks like a tramp. I recommend foster homes as soon as possible."

"Hey, look," I interrupted, "Dad is coming back on Thursday at the latest, and we got cases of food downstairs. We just don't happen to keep it in the cupboard."

I ran downstairs, got the last case of beans, and lugged it back to the kitchen. "Look at this," I said, "our whole basement is full of food." I didn't think they'd go downstairs to find out, seeing they'd have to step over part of the lawnmower engine to get there. It was a lie about there being more food downstairs, but I figured it was just as wrong for them to barge in with their clipboards and start making plans about shipping us to other homes.

"Who could we use?" Miss McCormack asked.

"How many children are there?" he asked.

"Just the three."

"The Johnson family could take one, Rosettis will take the girl, and Palmer might take the oldest boy."

I figured I had to shout to get them to hear me. "My dad said we could definitely expect him by Thursday. See, what happened was his manifold went out on the truck, and that caused his Bendix spring to break. He explained it all to me when he phoned me last night."

I rattled on, using words I'd learned at Olson's Garage. Mr. Ackley didn't seem to hear me, but finally Miss McCormack said, "He says his father is coming back on Thursday."

"I guess we can wait till then," he said.

They went to the car and wrote on their clipboards and then drove off. I knew they'd be back.

I knew what was coming. They were going to split us up and put us in three different homes, homes where we'd have hot cereal for breakfast and casseroles for supper. They wouldn't know that sometimes Ryan would wake up crying for Mom in the middle of the night, but if you went in and touched his forehead for a while, he'd fall asleep again. They wouldn't know that Jill didn't like corn. It didn't matter how often you said it was good for her, she wouldn't eat it—not plain, not creamed, and not on the cob. There were things about them only I knew, and if we were separated, we'd stop being a family. I couldn't let that happen. Dad put me in charge, not them.

I'd told so many people that Dad was coming home on Thursday that I almost believed it myself. But when Thursday morning came, I knew we had to do something or we'd wind up in foster homes, and be visited every week by Miss McCormack, not because she cared about us, but because the county was paying her to evaluate conditions.

I got Ryan and Jill up early. While they were eating their toast and peanut butter, I turned off the TV and told them what was going to happen to us if we didn't leave town. "They want to put us in different homes. If they do that, maybe we'll never see each other again."

Ryan looked like he was going to cry.

"Hey, don't worry, I won't let 'em do that, but we've got to leave town today. How'd you like to go to California?"

"Is that where Dad is?" Ryan asked.

Jill looked at me to see if I'd lie.

I would. "Yeah, he's there. He wants us to come and meet him."

"I'm supposed to do a report today for school," he said.

"Bring it with you. You can give it in California when we get there."

We went downstairs and got our camping gear and packed some food in our packs, plus a hatchet, matches, and a flashlight, along with our clothes. Then we took ropes and tied everything to our bikes.

We left about eleven that morning. On our way out of town I stopped at a few places and collected on my paper route.

The night before, when I'd thought about us leaving, I'd pictured us catching fish and eating berries and trapping animals for food on the way to California. But things never work out the way you picture them. We had to go slow because the chain on Ryan's bike kept coming off. Finally we had to take it in to get it fixed. So by three in the afternoon, we were still in town, surrounded by motels and fast-food stores. There were no trees to chop and no fish and no berries.

When the wind blows in Wyoming during the day, it's one thing, but at night in October, that's another thing entirely. If you don't know about Wyoming wind, you don't know what it's like to have nature ticked off at you. Just before dark we stopped at a city park. There were several McDonald's boxes lying around, and some other paper stashed in a trash can. We burned them to heat our can of pork and beans. We ate quickly. The beans on the bottom were burnt, and the ones on top barely warm. They tasted terrible. To make our meal a little better, I ran and bought fresh apple pies from McDonald's. Then we went to a shopping center and walked around until it closed.

It was a cold night. To keep warm we zipped two of our sleeping bags together, and all three of us crawled into it. It was tight but warm. Jill's hair tickled my nose.

We fell asleep.

Sometime during the night, we woke up with a flashlight shining in our eyes. "What are you kids doing here?" a cop asked.

"We're sleeping out," I said. "It's okay with our parents. We do it all the time."

"You can't stay overnight in this park."

We put on our shoes, rolled up our sleeping bags, and threw everything back into the packs.

The cop stood and watched us, then walked over to his car and picked up the mike for his two-way radio.

"I just found three kids sleeping in the park. You got anything on any runaways?"

"Run!" I whispered sharply to Ryan and Jill.

He saw us leaving. "Stop!" he called out.

Jill fell down. I stopped and helped her up. She put her arm around me while we continued across the street. I could hear the cop starting his car.

We ran through McDonald's parking lot, across another street, through one yard, along a fenceline for a while, and then into another yard. We found a garage door open and ran in and quietly closed the overhead door and waited.

There was a small window on the garage door. I kept watch. Jill quietly opened the door to the station wagon parked in the garage, and she and Ryan crawled in the back.

The police car passed the street twice, shining his spotlight on everything as he passed. After a few minutes, he quit circling the block.

I left Ryan and Jill and went back to see if I could find our gear. I saw the cop packing everything into his trunk. He parked behind a building to wait for us. After a few minutes, he tired of his game and drove away.

I went back to the garage. We stayed there until it began to get gray outside.

California seemed a long way off.

* * * * * * * * * * * * *

In the morning we slipped out of the garage and went to McDonald's for breakfast—Ryan and Jill needed the assurance of the familiar plastic and cardboard and Ronald McDonald to make them feel at home. There wasn't much money left, so I told them I wasn't hungry.

All the time they were eating, I kept telling them about California, and about the beaches and oranges, and about going swimming any time we wanted.

They believed me.

By the time we were through, we were feeling good again. I had a plan. We'd walk to the truckstop on the edge of town and tell them about Dad, how he was a trucker too, and because truckers stick together, one of them would give us a ride to California. We bundled up and started walking, but we had to stop every few blocks to warm up because of the wind.

It was almost noon by the time we got there. We sat at a booth and ordered two bowls of chili. I figured I could just eat some crackers and get by.

After we finished one tray of crackers, I went to another table and asked a trucker if we could have his. He nodded his head.

"My dad's a trucker too," I said. "You ever heard of him? Hank Pepper's his name."

"Can't say I have."

"He drives for Mayflower, goes all over the country. He went to Maine once. Where you going?"

"Oregon."

"Can we get a ride with you?"

He looked at Jill and Ryan. "Running away from home, huh?"

"Gosh, no. See, our mom moved there, and she wrote us a letter and told us she'd finally gotten an apartment, and said we should move out with her."

"But she didn't send any bus money?" he asked.

I paused. "Well, sure, but it got stolen from my locker at school."

"Phone her and she'll send some more."

"Well, that's just it, because I can't remember where she said she moved to, so we don't know how to contact her."

"What town in Oregon did she go to? You can call the police and they'll find her for you."

"That's just it. I don't remember what town in Oregon it is."

"Then it wouldn't do any good for me to take you there, would it?"

"Oh, once we got to Oregon, we'd know."

I paused, and he grinned. "Gotcha," he said, his toothpick waving in his mouth as he talked. He got up and paid his bill and left. I made sure he didn't stop at a pay phone and call the cops before he left.

Another trucker finished his meal. I sent Ryan over for his tray of crackers.

A few minutes later I looked out to see a cop car pulling into the parking lot near an outdoor phone booth. The first guy we'd talked to stepped out of his truck to talk to him.

"Let's get out of here!" I pulled Jill and Ryan with me, through the kitchen and out the back door.

We ran full speed to the end of the parking lot and into a vacant lot.

We kept moving. Finally I saw a large water drainpipe, tall enough to walk through if you bent over. It went underneath the highway. I found some wooden crates we could sit on, so we went in and rested.

We waited till dark. It started to snow. I decided on a plan. We went back to the shopping center.

"Look for a car either with the keys in it or else unlocked," I said.

"What for?" Jill asked.

"We're going to steal a car," I said.

"We are?" Jill asked.

"Somebody's not going to like that," Ryan said.

"If the caseworkers get us, we'll never see each other again. Do you want that to happen?"

He shook his head.

"All right then. Find a car."

We started walking slowly through the parking lot.

"Here's one that's not locked!" Ryan yelled.

"Quiet!" I whispered loudly.

We hurried to the car and looked in.

"But there's no keys in it," Ryan complained. "You need keys."

"I'll hot wire it," I said.

"What does that mean?" Jill asked.

"For crying out loud, Jill. Don't you know what hot wiring means? It means you start the car without keys."

I had Ryan and Jill keep watch while I got in the car. I stared at the dashboard and wished I knew what to do. I tried to start it without the key, but it wouldn't work.

After a few minutes Jill complained. "It doesn't look like you're doing anything except staring."

I decided hot wiring must involve something under the hood. I stepped out and after struggling for a few minutes finally got the hood open.

I stared at the engine. There were so many parts.

"Why don't you do something?" Jill asked.

I looked at her.

"You don't really know how to hot wire a car, do you."

"It's different with a Ford," I said, slamming the hood shut.

"It's okay. I'm glad you don't know how."

I felt like a failure.

She put her hand on my shoulder. "Hey, it's okay. Don't worry so much."

I felt better. She could always do that to me.

There was no place to go except home. When we got there, we didn't put on any lights because we were afraid the cops or Mr. Ackley would be checking the house, looking for us. The house was cold, and the furnace didn't work. I figured somebody'd turned off our gas. We paddled around in the dark until all the blinds were shut, then pulled the TV set into the bedroom, where the three of us huddled together and ate peanut butter and beans and watched TV till we fell asleep.

I was the first to wake up in the morning. I unraveled Jill's hand on my arm, and Ryan's leg from on top of me, and looked outside. It had snowed a couple of inches during the night.

I looked at Jill. She was the prettiest girl in the world, but I never told her that. For one thing, she was always a pain when we were younger, because she always told on me. The first words she ever said, according to our mother, were "Dimmy did it." Mom told us that whenever she said that, I would turn to her and scowl and say, "Dumb dumb Dill."

That morning I pictured myself protecting her and Ryan from life's harsh realities. In the end, they were the ones who saved me from self-destruction.

Ryan woke up. "I like all of us sleeping together," he said.

"Yeah, but we can't do it all the time," I said.

"Why not?"

"Because Jill's a girl."

"So what?"

"It's just not done." I looked at Jill sleeping. "You're too young to understand."

"Let's wake her up," Ryan said.

I picked up my pillow and dropped it on her head. She mumbled something and rolled over on her side.

"Ryan," I whispered, "now you do it."

He hesitated.

"It's okay, go ahead." I said.

He did. She awoke and sat up. While she yawned, I tossed a pillow at her. She picked it back up and threw it at me, then jumped at me and knocked me down on the bed and sat on me and started hitting me with the pillow. I was laughing so hard I couldn't fight back.

"Ryan, help me!"

"How?"

"Hit her with the other pillow!"

Never in his whole life had Ryan wanted to hurt anyone. When we were very young, Mom would give gold stars to the child who was the most obedient that week. I never got the gold star. Jill got it some of the time, when she was not hanging around me, but mostly Ryan got it. I used to call him Gold Star.

Now he had a problem. He could help me only by hitting Jill with a pillow.

"Ryan! Please!" I giggled.

He hesitated, then picked up the pillow and hit Jill with it, knocking her off me.

"All right you two!" she yelled, laughing at the same time.

What a mess we made. By the time we were through, the pillows had ripped and there was a cloud of feathers every time we hit each other. But we didn't care anymore about the house.

Sometimes your mind takes a picture and freezes it, along with all the emotions and textures of a moment. There is such a picture in my mind of the three of us standing on the bed giggling uncontrollably, feathers floating everywhere. Jumping on the bed, holding hands in a circle.

The last of a family circle.

After we'd scattered feathers all over, the bed frame broke from too much jumping. We sat on the mattress, now on the floor, and ate peanut butter with a knife out of the jar and watched Saturday cartoons.

About ten o'clock a car pulled up. I looked out and saw Mr. Ackley and Miss McCormack coming up the walk.

"Get dressed!" I ordered, turning off the TV. "We'll have to run for it."

I'd already dressed, but they scurried around in their pajamas hunting for their clothes among the rubble of feathers.

"Hurry up!"

There was a knock at the door.

Jill found her things and ran into the bathroom to change. Ryan stood there in the middle of the room, looking dazed.

"What's wrong?" I asked him.

"I can't find one of my shoes."

The knock became louder.

"For crying out loud! Where did you put 'em last night?"

"I don't know."

"Hurry up! If they catch us, they'll throw us in jail!"

I frantically helped him look for his shoe. While I was moving the mattress, I accidentally bumped part of the frame, which collapsed even further, making a loud crash.

"We know you're in there!" I heard Mr. Ackley shout. "Let us in!"

Jill came in dressed.

"He lost one of his shoes," I told her. "Try to find it, while I go stall 'em."

Mr. Ackley was pounding on the door.

"Just a minute," I shouted.

I took as long as possible to open the door a crack, but I left the chain on.

"What do you want?" I asked Mr. Ackley.

"Is your father here?"

"Yeah—he got in late last night. You know that Bendix gear I was telling you about, well, wouldn't you know it, it went out again on him. I asked him about it, and he said, it's just something that happens on some models of Mack trucks, especially that particular model . . ."

"We want to talk to him."

"He's sleeping."

"Well, can you get him up?"

"He doesn't like to be woken up when he comes back from a long trip."

"When will he be awake?"

"This afternoon sometime."

"Can you unlock the door?"

"I'm not supposed to let strangers in the house."

"I think you're lying about your father being here," Mr. Ackley said.

"If you want to wait in the car, I'll let you know when he wakes up."

"We're going to the police," Mr. Ackley said. "They'll be able to get him up."

"Wait, don't do that. I'll go see if I can wake him up. It may take a while though."

I walked slowly down the hall until Mr. Ackley couldn't see me, then ran into the bedroom. Ryan was still standing there, one shoe on, and Jill was on her hands and knees feeling inch by inch for the shoe.

"Forget about the shoe! Go out the back now! And hurry! I'll meet you by the tree fort in a minute."

I watched them leave, then walked back to the front door.

"My dad says he doesn't want to see anybody for a while. He's sick. He says he's been throwing up all night. He's afraid you might catch it."

"You're lying," Mr. Ackley said.

I shrugged my shoulders. "Okay then—but don't blame me if you come down with it. I'll go get him."

I walked slowly out of his sight, then ran out the back door.

Mr. Ackley didn't trust anybody. He'd just sent Miss McCormack to the back. She watched me as I ran down the stairs and past her through the yard. "He's running away!" she called out.

I caught up with Ryan and Jill at our favorite hideout, a large tree in a neighbor's yard.

Ryan was standing on one foot crying. Not a sound from him really, just silent tears rolling down his face.

"What's wrong?"

"He wet his pants," Jill said.

I looked. She was right.

"He was scared about being thrown in jail," she said. "That's all."

It was a mark against his manhood, and we all knew it.

"Sure. Hey, Ryan, it's okay."

He shook his head slowly.

"No, really, Ryan, it's okay," Jill said. "We understand. We're scared too. Hey, don't cry, Ryan."

"Are you cold?" I asked him.

He shook his head.

"It's warm now, but it'll get cold," I said. "Hey, Ryan, c'mon. It's no big thing. You gotta quit crying now, okay?"

We stood there for a while, telling Ryan it was okay. It started to snow again. Ryan started to shiver and we had nowhere to go. We were beaten and we knew it.

We walked to Kevin's back door and knocked. His mother answered the door and invited us in. Inside the house everything seemed so ordinary. It seemed a miracle that some people could live like that.

I went to Kevin privately and told him about Ryan. He gave us an old pair of jeans and some underwear for him to wear. TV cartoons were on. We sat down to watch. Kevin's mother asked if we'd like some pancakes.

At breakfast his parents didn't ask questions, and we didn't say much of anything. We just ate and ate. But when Kevin's mother put the second load of pancakes on Ryan's plate, she touched his shoulder the way mothers do. I was sorry she'd done it, because he broke down and started crying.

He cried a long time. After a while, we got the story out clear enough so they could understand. Kevin's dad called the bishop. The bishop came and took me to his office at church, and left Ryan and Jill at Kevin's so they could watch Saturday cartoons.

I told the bishop everything; then he got on the

phone and made five or six phone calls. By the time the morning was over, I'd talked to Mr. Ackley and Miss McCormack. The bishop made me apologize.

The bishop asked if we'd like to stay with Kevin's parents for a while. He said it was okay with Miss McCormack.

"It'll just be for a little while," I told Ryan and Jill, "just till Dad gets back."

"He's not coming back," Jill later said just to me, "and you know it."

CHAPTER TWO

     After Hank phoned, I stewed for a couple of days and then called Jill in Burley, Idaho.

  "Hank called me. He wants to see us."

  She paused. "Who's Hank?"

  "Our father."

  "Daddy phoned?" she asked excitedly. "Where is he?"

  "Buffalo, Wyoming."

  "How does he sound?"

  "All right, I guess."

  "Jimmy, do you want to see him?"

  "No."

  "Why not?"

  There was a long silence, and then I said, "I'm afraid."

  "But we have to, don't we?" she said.

  "Do we?"

  "He's our father. We have to see him when he asks us. Maybe he's sick or something."

  I sighed. "Okay."

  We made plans. I would fly from Los Angeles to Idaho, and then we'd drive their family car to Buffalo.

  "Jill, I'll need some help with this."

  "We'll have time to get our heads on straight during the drive."

  "If we wait for me to get my head on straight, we'll end up taking a ferry across the Bering Strait."

  We said good-bye. Just before I was about to make my plane reservations, the phone rang. It was a reporter from the "National Inquirer," wanting to do an article about me.

  "What kind of article?" I asked.

"About your growing up. We'll talk to high school friends, get their impressions of what you were like. Talk to your parents, you know, human interest."

"I've seen some of the garbage you write. I'm not interested."

"Look, we're going to do the article one way or the other. It'd be better if you cooperated."

I hung up, my forehead beaded with sweat. What if they find out about my father?

We stayed with Kevin's family for a few weeks, then they were transferred to Alaska by the Air Force. The bishop tried to get someone in the ward to take us, but he didn't have much luck—because they knew us. Finally he got permission to send us to Idaho as extras to the Lamanite placement program.

"But we're not Indians," I said.

"Sometimes we send a few special cases to Idaho."

The bus trip to Idaho was a grand adventure for us. They'd given us money, and we bought a large supply of junk food to eat along the way.

I remember our night on the bus. It was late, and everyone was asleep but Jill and me. I was just opening a large bag of Krunchies while she looked thoughtfully out the window.

"Whataya thinking about, Jillsy?"

"Look at the stars," she said.

I leaned over and looked. "Yeah—what about 'em?"

"There's so many."

"Sure are—want any Krunchies?"

"You're hopeless," she said.

"What's wrong?"

"You don't understand anything."

"Understand what? That there's a lot of stars? Cripes, Jillsy, everybody knows that."

She turned away from me. "You're too immature to understand."

"I'm as mature as you are any day. Go ahead, tell me what you're thinking about."

"It was a feeling I had, looking at the stars. It's like they're trying to say something."

I took a large handful of Krunchies, stuffed them into my mouth, then leaned over and stared out the window. "Yeah? What are they saying to you, Jillsy?"

"Just forget it, okay?" she said.

"Sure thing—want any Krunchies?"

"You're about as deep thinking as a mouse."

"Well, if you'd quit talking in riddles. Why don't you quit beating around the bush?"

"You're such a retard. Haven't you ever looked at the stars at night and got goose bumps just thinking about, well, life?"

"Life?" I teased. "You're thinking about life? What's there to think about?"

"Things like—I wonder where Mom is."

"She's dead."

"But where is she? I don't mean her body. Where is she?"

"How should I know? What I'd like to know is, where's Dad?"

"I dreamed about us once, you and me and Ryan."

She was serious. I stopped a handful of Krunchies midway to my mouth as a token of respect for deep thought.

"What happened in your dream?"

"We died. At least I think we were dead."

"How did we die? In a gunfight, I bet. The first famous brother-sister gang in history. I can see it now. The Pepper Gang. Take that, POW, and that, BANG. Ahhh! They got me, Jillsy!" I fell limp on her shoulder, gasping, my tongue hanging out. Then I sprang up. "How about it? Shall we get off the bus and hitchhike to California and steal avocados?"

She smiled, but only a little. "I sort of want to be good," she confessed.

"A religious girl?" I teased her.

"What's so bad about that?"

"Like Kevin and his family? All they do is pray. Pray in the morning, pray at night, pray whenever they eat. What are they so scared about they got to pray all the time? I say don't bother God until things are really scuzzy, then go to it."

"Did you see the way Kevin's father treated his wife?"

"Yeah, what about it?"

"He really loves her."

"So maybe he does. She's not too bad."

"He respects her."

"Ah, come on. I suppose he's your ideal man? I bet he wears a tie in the shower. Anyway, tell me your dream."

"We were walking in a forest, and we came upon a clearing and there he was."

"Who was?"

"God, I think."

I paused, then asked quietly, "Yeah? What'd He say?"

"Nothing."

"Nothing? He sounds like that school librarian who knew everything, but every time you asked a question, he'd say, 'You can look that up yourself.'"

"Don't make fun of my dream," she said. I backed off and tried to look serious while she continued. "It was more of a feeling I got. A feeling that God cares. That's all that happened—a strong feeling that God cares about us."

I took another handful of Krunchies. "Sure, why not? If He cares about the sparrows, like they say in church, then He's got to care about us. For one thing, we're a lot bigger than a stupid sparrow."

She turned away. "Why do you always have to make fun of everything? We used to be able to talk about serious things."

"It's not me that's changing, you know. It's you. You're changing. You're getting so moody."

She stared silently out the window as shadows of the

night passed us by. I sat and philosophically munched Krunchies.

Suddenly she started crying. When she was younger and did that, I could get away with putting my arm around her shoulder and giving her a hug. But somewhere lately we'd come to a time when we couldn't do that. Now we hardly touched each other at all except when she slugged me. "They're going to break us up, Jimmy. I know they will. We're not going to be a family anymore."

"I won't let 'em break us up. I promise."

"They'll do whatever they want to."

"Look, Jillsy, I've been thinking. Okay, we stay in Idaho a few weeks, but then, whataya say, we run away for California—you and me and Ryan. I'll get a job and make good money, and we'll get a place by the ocean, like on TV, and everything'll be fine. I'll take care of you and Ryan."

"That'd be nice. You're so much fun to be with—sometimes."

"It never gets cold in California, and if you want any fruit, you just go outside and pick it. And it never snows, so you don't have to buy coats."

"You're not just talking like Daddy used to, are you?"

"No, I promise it'll happen. I'll take care of you."

She seemed better after that, and soon she went to sleep. Her head lay on my shoulder, and even though I was awake and had to go to the bathroom in the back of the bus, I didn't move for a long time.

The next morning we both woke up at the same time. She stretched and looked over at me. I was still holding the half-eaten bag. "Hey, don't hog all the Krunchies," she said with a mischievous grin, grabbing for the bag.

It was our last tickling contest.

The bus driver made us pick up all the Krunchies we spilled.

* * * * * * * * * * * *

Jill was right about one thing—they split us up.

The man from LDS Social Services who picked us up at the bus station, Brother Bateman, explained they were going to put us in three different homes. We would end up in towns strung along the Snake River, Jill in Twin Falls, me fifty miles to the east in Burley, and Ryan sixty miles from me, in American Falls.

They took us to an office and asked us a lot of questions; then they took us to a doctor and made us wait in a sitting room, and then made us wait in separate rooms. At first they kept saying the doctor would see us right away, but later they said there was an emergency at the hospital and the doctor had to leave, so we were each sitting there in our underwear in three different rooms, waiting. After fifteen minutes, I decided I'd had it, so I put on my clothes and started knocking on doors with a special code we had. I found Jill and told her to get dressed, and then we found Ryan. We started to walk out of the office, but the nurse told us we couldn't leave, so we went back into Ryan's room and started rummaging through the medical supplies.

Ryan was very quiet that day. I worried the most about him. For his benefit more than anything else I had us sit down on the floor, and I found a sharp knife and made a small cut on my thumb.

"Now you do it," I said, handing the knife to Jill.

"What for?"

"It's a ceremony," I said.

She made a cut. I touched my thumb to hers.

"Now, Ryan, you make a cut."

I was surprised, but he did it.

I took his thumb and touched it to ours.

"This means they'll never separate us. We did it on the thumb because that's what you use when you hitch-hike. We're in a special club now, just the three of us. Ryan, I know you might get scared being alone, but we got common blood, and no matter what they do to us, we'll be together. This is a real serious promise we're making. What we're promising is that if it really gets too bad for one of us, then the one who's hurting has to write the other two and tell 'em, and we'll come and, if we have to, we'll run away again, all three of us. Agreed?"

Ryan solemnly nodded his head.

"Don't be so quiet all the time, Ryan. Say it."

"I agree."

"Jill?"

"I agree."

"Okay. Now, Ryan, I got to talk to you. You keep things inside. You got to let 'em out once in a while. All the time you're trying to be good, and that's okay I guess, but if you feel bad, let it out. Look, it's all right once in a while to go turn over somebody's garbage can, or put soap on their car windows, or just let somebody know you feel rotten. Don't let them box you in. If you hurt, let somebody know it. You know, like me. I know you don't like the way I mouth off sometimes, but it feels good to let it out. And if it gets too bad, just call me and I'll come and we'll all go to California and live. Okay?"

He swallowed hard, fought back the tears, and silently nodded.

I knew it was a corny thing to do, and cutting our thumbs didn't really change a thing, and besides I'd read it in *Tom Sawyer* anyway, but Ryan needed something, and it was the only thing I could think of at the time.

A few minutes later a nurse came in and gasped, seeing us sitting on the floor with blood on us and me holding a scalpel. When she finally realized we were all right, she chewed us out. She got Brother Bateman, and he came and told us he was ashamed of us. I didn't care what he thought. The important thing was to help Ryan.

The doctor eventually came back and gave us the exam. Then we were driven back to LDS Social Services, where they split us up into three different cars to be driven to our foster homes.

Poor Ryan. He looked dazed and alone in the parking lot just before we left. I walked up to him and showed him my thumb with the cut. "Remember now, anytime you can't stand it, just let me know."

He nodded and started crying. I hugged him and told him it was going to be all right.

Even Jill let me hug her before they split us up.

I was assigned to Logan and Zinia Larsen, sober people past middle-age with their family all grown up and away from home.

Brother Bateman delivered me to their home about two in the afternoon. It was a small house, stuck in the country a few miles from Burley. The Snake River ran through their farm. They grew mostly potatoes. Many years ago their house had been smaller, but year after year as their family grew it had been added on, so now one walked through a series of small dark rooms that wound out like tentacles from an octopus. The whole house was like a maze.

Brother Bateman introduced me to Zinia Larsen, a thin woman with steel gray eyes and dull brown hair done up in a tight bun. She wore thick, dark horn-rimmed glasses. Her face was bony and creased with deep lines, untouched with makeup. From the conversation with the social worker, I gathered she had several Indian kids stay there before me. She showed me to my room. It was small and square and sparse.

The three of us returned to the kitchen, and she served us each a slice of homemade bread and a glass of milk. It was the best bread I'd ever eaten in my life, home baked and fresh from the oven.

Brother Bateman kept praising her, thanking her for being willing to take in foster kids, but she parried each compliment and turned it away, so none of it reached her. I was to learn that Zinia did not accept praise. For her, it was enough to do something out of duty.

Then Brother Bateman left, and I was all alone. We spent the first afternoon in what Zinia called orientation. "This is the bathroom," she said slowly and carefully as if I'd never seen one before. "Do you know the proper way to use a toilet?"

I started to laugh, but one severe look from her shut me up.

She advanced to the toilet. "Number one: lift up the seat. Number two: use the facility. Number three: put the seat down. Number four: do not use too much paper. Number five: flush. Number six: wash hands with soap and water. Number seven: don't dawdle in the bathroom. Others may be waiting to use it. Those are the seven steps to using the toilet."

I stared in disbelief as she presented her lecture. She turned to face the bathroom door, on which was fastened a poster. "These seven steps will always be listed here. Each time you come in, you should go through the list until it becomes second nature to you. Now, let's turn our attention to the shower."

There was a list of six things for the shower, also posted.

"When we finish our showers, we don't leave our dirty clothes in the bathroom, do we?"

"No," I said.

"Why don't we?"

She answered her own question. "Because that'd make somebody else clean it up. In our family, everyone takes care of his own things. Now this is what we do after we take a shower. First, we turn off the water very tight, because if the water drips it wastes energy. Next we get out and dry ourselves thoroughly but quickly. And again, we don't dawdle in the bathroom, do we. Then we take the soap tray and dump any excess water that might've fallen into it. That will keep the soap from dissolving. Next we take our towel and hang it up."

She turned around quickly and nearly knocked me

off my feet as she headed to the wall. "Do you see this hook?"

I nodded my head.

"This is your hook."

Oh boy, I thought sarcastically, I get my own hook.

"This hook is where you will hang your towel. I've even written your name on the hook. This is a special place for your towel. It shouldn't be found anywhere but here."

I was getting a headache keeping my jokes to myself.

"Now let's go to your room."

The bedroom lists were posted on the inside of the closet, giving instructions about matching my dirty socks before I put them in the hamper so she wouldn't have to match them after they were washed. Instructions about making the bed every morning before breakfast except on Monday, when I should take the sheets off the bed and deposit them in the hamper for washing. Instructions on what to do with soil-caked jeans. Instructions and lists.

At six her husband, Logan, came home. I was in the kitchen helping her peel carrots when he entered. He was a large, raw-boned man. He took off his boots and overalls in a room off the kitchen, put on another pair of pants and shoes, and came in.

"Supper'll be ready in a minute," Zinia said.

He nodded his head, stared silently at me, shook his head, and went into the bathroom.

She directed me to put the food on the table. We sat down and waited for her husband. He came in and sat down, bowed his head, and offered the blessing on the food. We ate silently, except for me slurping my soup.

"His name is Jimmy," she said.

"He's not Indian."

"No."

"They don't send whites out here unless something's wrong with 'em."

"He's okay. He'll work around the place."

"You always say that, and it always ends up costing me more, what with them losing my tools, and breaking my equipment, and forgetting their chores. I'd be better off without 'em." He turned to me. "What's wrong with you?"

I looked up, uncertain of what to say.

"He was abandoned, he and his brother and sister."

Turning to me again, he asked, "You know anything about farming?"

"No," I said.

"That's what I figured."

Our meal was soup and bread and carrot sticks. I would have liked another bowl but was too timid to ask. She soon whisked the food off the table and had me help with the dishes. Logan went to the living room to read the paper.

After I finished helping, she said I could do whatever I wanted for forty-five minutes, before we went through the countdown for bed. I asked if I could go outside for a while. Permission was granted. She showed me the large bell she'd ring when it was time for me to come in again.

Finally freed from prison, I ran from the house along a path lit by the light from the moon. There was a large tree a few minutes away. I climbed it and sat on a branch. From there I could see the gray metallic reflection of the moon off the Snake River.

I figured I was alone. I practiced mimicking Zinia's instructions about using the bathroom. Then I looked down. A guy my age, wearing a sweat shirt and baggy sweat pants, was looking up at me.

"Nice talk," he said.

"I didn't think anybody'd hear."

"God hears," he said. "He hears what everybody says, even swearing."

"Then He ought to be used to it after all these years," I countered.

"You're an Indian, aren't you, and you're staying with the Larsens."

"I'm not an Indian."

"Why do you think they call it the Indian placement program? You got to be an Indian to come here."

"I'm not an Indian."

"What are you then?"

"I'm a special case."

He guffawed. "Special case—sure thing, Chief," he said, chuckling to himself.

"Don't call me chief."

"What grade you in?"

"I'm a freshman in high school."

"We don't have freshmen here. Freshmen are ninth graders. And ninth graders go to junior high school. Don't say you're a freshman. Say you're a ninth grader, 'cause that's what you are."

"And what are you, a fifth grader?"

"I'm a freshman too."

I jumped out of the tree to get a closer look. He was shorter than me, had a smart-aleck look I liked. "Do you always wear your pajamas outdoors?" I asked.

"Pajamas!" he roared. "That's all you know. This is my uniform. I run cross-country and track."

"You're too fat to run. I can outrun you any day. Indians run like the wind. Everybody knows that."

"I thought you weren't an Indian."

I grinned. "It comes and goes. When I run, I'm an Indian, and I run on wing-éd feet."

"Wing-éd feet!" He laughed.

"It's true."

"Want to race?" he asked.

"Sure, why not? But not tonight. I'm not ready. When I run, I have to wear sunglasses as a heat shield. See, I run so fast there's a red glow around me."

He laughed. "You're really a cornball, you know that?"

"How far you want to go? How about if we run to Twin Falls and back?"

"What's so great about Twin Falls?"

"That's where my sister is."

"An Indian maiden," he said.

"Nobody makes wisecracks about my sister while I'm around."

"Okay, okay."

"Anyway," I said, "it'll take me that far to get warmed up. I hate short distances."

"Listen to the wind blow," he howled. "On wing-éd feet."

"What's it like at school?" I asked.

He laughed. "It's the pits. Some of my teachers taught my parents when *they* were in school. Teachers get brittle when they get old—like dried-out twigs. If they fall down, they snap in two and break. All my teachers are like that. You'll hate it, believe me."

"I believe it."

"All the girls are ugly—the farmers send their pigs to school and keep their daughters at home. What's your sister like?"

"She wouldn't be interested in you," I said.

"Why not?"

"She's got good taste."

Off in the distance I heard the cowbell. It was Zinia's signal.

"I gotta go. Tell me your name."

"Scott Allison. And yours?"

"Jimmy Pepper." I started running away.

"Are you sure it isn't Iron Cloud or Broken Arrow?" he shouted.

I stopped to call back. "Hey, tomorrow night at this same time, you be here and we'll run that race, okay?"

Zinia rang the bell again. I ran home.

"James," she said unhappily as I came puffing into the yard, "do you know how many times I rang the bell?"

"Three times," I said.

"That's right—three times—five minutes apart. I should never have to ring it more than once. You come running when you hear the bell."

"Yes."

"Well, come in now. Bedtime is nine o'clock in this house. But before we go to bed, there are certain steps we take—things that preserve our health and assure us a proper rest." She handed me a list for bed. First she went over it in agonizing detail. She warned me about drinking too much just before bed. She showed me how to brush my teeth, how to squeeze a toothpaste tube from the bottom up, how to put the top back on. She warned me about not reading in bed after nine, and about saying my own prayers just before I climbed into bed. She made me tack the list on the bulletin board above my tiny desk. I looked at that list every night for the next four years, and even now find myself going over it in my head each night.

That first night in bed I felt the cut on my thumb and imagined Ryan and Jill touching theirs. I hoped it helped them get through their first night. I lay awake thinking of how the three of us would soon move to California.

Zinia drove me to school the first day. We walked into the principal's office and she introduced me, then went to his office to talk privately with him.

While I waited, I looked at an old picture hanging on the wall—George Washington crossing the Delaware. The others in the boat probably thought he was stupid to stand up, but he was their boss, so they just couldn't yell at him, "Hey Dumbo, sit down!" They kept their comments to themselves the way I was learning to do around Zinia.

In a few minutes, Zinia left and the principal took me down to the guidance counselor. The halls were long and hollow sounding, and passing each door, we could hear the buzz of education.

The guidance counselor was Miss Crampton. She looked at a piece of paper. "We're in the middle of things now, so it may be a little hard to get you in the classes you want. What classes do you want?"

"Easy classes," I said.

"Like what?"

"Auto repair," I said.

"That's not offered in junior high school."

"Art."

"Full. What else?"

"Wood shop," I said.

"Full."

"Just choose some easy classes for me. I'm just going to be here a short time; then my brother and sister and me are going to California."

A few minutes later, she handed me a schedule.

During lunch, I ate alone.

"Hi, Chief," Scott said, coming up behind me and slapping me on the back.

"Don't call me chief."

He reached over and scooped up the tiny bit of whipped cream on my dessert with his finger and ate it. I pushed his hand away.

"Why don't you join band?"

"Are you in it?"

"In it? I'm the star!"

I held back a grin. "That's one reason for not joining."

"I'm serious. It's a lot of fun. You can play the drums. Indians are good with drums, right?" He reached over to grab my cake.

I picked up the knife on my tray and pointed it at him. "They're also good with knives."

He backed off about my dessert. "Sorry, but hey, I'm serious about band. You and me, we'd have a good time.

Think about it. A band with forty girls and fifteen guys. And most of the guys are strange—the kind that only talk about math homework. They all think they're going into the space program. So we got two or three normal guys to forty girls. And we don't have homework, and you get to make noise, and with that many people, the director can't know who's serious about music and who's just messing around, so he gives an automatic B to everybody. And sometimes we go on trips. Hey, whataya say? I don't ask just anybody to join band, you know."

I enrolled in band.

Starting over in a new school was a lonely experience. To make matters worse, Scott wasn't in any of my classes except for band.

On my second day of class, the teacher gave us a reading assignment, but everyone was visiting with everyone else. She looked up from her book and warned, "Quiet down, class. I don't want to hear another peep from you."

They quieted down. In a tiny voice, I gave my impression of a baby chicken. "Peep."

The whole class started laughing. The teacher looked sternly over at me, and then her frown broke, and she started laughing too.

I looked at the cute girl who sat next to me. She was smiling at me. I winked at her. She winked back.

"I think our new student is a comedian," the teacher said. "Jimmy, we must have it quiet now. But you know, the school is having a talent show soon. Why don't you try out for it?"

They were all smiling at me.

"Maybe I will," I said, happy for the first time in a long time.

I spent the next few days stealing jokes from every place I could think of. I checked out every joke book I could find in the library and watched as much TV as I could. I read every back issue of *Boys' Life* that Scott had. And then I practiced in front of a mirror in the bathroom, which was not at all pleasing to Zinia. But she seemed to sense it was important to me, although for what purpose she had no idea.

And then came the school talent show. I walked on carrying a stool and sat down. It had been raining all day, so I had decided to start with a rain joke I'd stolen from a joke book. "Hey, how about this rain? You know, we don't usually get this much rain. During the great flood, you know, the one you read about in the Bible, where it rained forty days and forty nights, this area got two-tenths of an inch."

They laughed.

Next a joke I'd stolen from a TV comedian. "Any parents out there have kids who've taken the Iowa tests? Thing I can't figure out is why we in Idaho have to take Iowa tests. Do you people have any idea some of the questions they ask in the Iowa tests?—What's the capital of Iowa? Who's the governor of Iowa? What's the largest city in Iowa? Strange thing is, kids from Iowa do so much better on it than kids from Idaho . . ."

They laughed.

The girls laughed too. I could see them smiling at me, hundreds of them. And guys too—laughing. And parents. It was important to be loved, especially by parents of daughters. And teachers. Teachers were important because they held life and death power over you in school. And they were laughing too.

They loved me.

It was the best feeling in the world. I wanted to be loved by everyone, to make people happy and have them approve of me. It was almost like they were all reaching out and touching me and I was touching them. Each laugh was love and warmth and tenderness.

I decided on my life's work.

I was going to be a comedian.

CHAPTER THREE

Jill and I didn't plan on leaving her home until she'd gotten her kids in bed after supper.

Just before we were ready, the phone rang. It was for me. "Alan Becker—I talked to you in L.A. about doing an article about you. A friend of mine and I are out here. Tomorrow we'll start talking to some locals about your background. I was wondering if I could come out and talk to you and your sister."

I hung up. An hour later we left for Wyoming. We drove for a couple of hours, then stopped for a snack in a nearly empty roadside cafe.

"They're going to find out about Hank's prison record," I said.

"So what? It was a long time ago."

"You don't know the way they can twist things. Maybe you shouldn't even be going there with me."

Jill shrugged. "I think you're being paranoid."

I bought an issue of the "National Inquirer" for her when I got gas.

"I see why you're worried," she said, a few minutes later.

We took off again. Jill fell asleep before very long. Like an owl, I came alive late at night. It was only me and the road and late-night radio.

And my thoughts.

Before that first year in Idaho, Christmas had been a time of great anticipation because my father, although he was often away from home driving, felt guilty enough at Christmas to overcompensate by giving too many toys and candy.

Seeing the preparations in the Larsen home, I naturally thought it'd be the same. Starting right after I arrived, Zinia turned out fruitcakes by the dozens.

Gradually I learned that none of it was for us. The fruitcakes were given to friends. After I'd tasted one, I wondered why she went to all the trouble. It was full of bitter-tasting fruit rinds dyed unnaturally ugly. One slice was all anyone should ever have in his entire life. The cookies were reserved for her grandchildren because they were too honest, and if you gave them a piece of fruitcake, they'd spit it out and say it was awful. And, of course, it was.

Two days before Christmas, the Larsen family members began to arrive. Fred was the oldest boy. He was at that time in his early thirties, with his hair nearly gone, especially along the top of his head, leaving only a few strands along the sides. He was already getting a paunch. He had graduated as an accountant and now worked for a firm in Denver. He liked telling people what was wrong with the government.

His wife's name was Margaret, and she always looked tired. They had three children in diapers. Their family took over my room, forcing me to sleep on the floor in the living room. Whenever I went to my room during the day to get some clothes, it smelled of diapers.

Logan and Zinia's next oldest was a daughter named Ruth. She stood six foot two and weighed a ton. Her husband was smaller than she was. He was one of the few Andrews in the world that nobody called Andy. He taught math in high school in Montana. He liked to talk about how low the salaries were and how little people valued teachers. Ruth pretty much ran Andrew. He changed the diapers of their two kids quite often.

The last one in the family was Rachel. She was a sophomore at Brigham Young University, engaged to be married in the summer. She brought along her future husband for Christmas. His name was Jeff, and he was from California and was studying to be a lawyer.

Rachel and Jeff were the only ones there who paid much attention to me, and they were the best looking of the lot.

Christmas began at five-thirty in the morning with little kids padding across my sleeping bag to the tree, giggling and laughing and playing with the things Santa had left unwrapped there. An hour later the parents and grandparents were coaxed into the room. Presents were passed around to each one. I had three presents.

There were planes and cars and games and candy—for the children.

I opened a present. It was a white shirt.

"Thanks," I said politely.

"That's for Sunday," Zinia said.

I nodded my head.

There were battery-powered boats for the bathtub and flashlights that glowed red and small puzzles—for the children.

I opened my second present. It was a pair of pajamas.

"Thank you," I said weakly.

"Now you won't have to go to bed in your underwear," Zinia said.

There were toy guns and felt-tipped darts for the dart board. There was what looked like a book but was made up of rolls of Life Savers—for the children.

I opened my third present—five pairs of black socks.

"Thanks," I whispered.

I sat and watched the others play with their toys and eat their Life Savers.

Zinia came out from the kitchen. "I know this will spoil our appetites for breakfast, but it's Christmas, and Christmas only comes once a year. Jimmy, pass around this plate of fruitcake."

Each one took a piece and politely nibbled on it, all ex-

cept Rachel's fiancé, who, being a stranger to the family
and wanting to please, took a hearty bite. After three
chews he realized what he'd done. I saw him hide the rest
of it under some wrapping.

The children then proceeded to wreck all their toys,
while the women retired to the kitchen to fix supper,
which was eight hours away. Fred and Andrew sat down
and talked about buying up gold. The kids were making
a horrible noise. Logan went to his shed to find a screw to
fix a kitchen chair. At least that's what he said, but it took
him a powerful long time to find one screw.

I sat in the living room and looked at my socks and
pajamas and wondered how Jill and Ryan were doing. I
went to a small office Logan had where there was a
phone. I sat down and called Ryan.

"How's it going?"

"I got a BB gun for Christmas!" he said excitedly.
"And a basketball and scout knife!"

"Hey, that's great."

"What did you get?" he asked.

"A lot of neat things too," I lied.

"And they let me drive their neighbors' snowmobile
yesterday."

"Hey, that's good."

"I'm a Blazer scout now. I'm trying to earn my
second-class rank."

"Good, Ryan. That's real good."

Next I phoned Jill.

"Next year maybe the three of us can spend Christmas by ourselves living in California," I said.

She paused. "Maybe longer than a year. I'd like to
graduate from high school first before we go it alone. But
then we will, the three of us, just like we talked about."

"If we can talk Ryan into it. You know, he's kind of a
pain. He'd be afraid of moving to California because he
might miss a scout meeting or something."

I told her how funny I was at the talent assembly. She

made me give my monologue to her on the phone. She giggled all the way through it.

Fred came in the room and grabbed the phone from me and put it up to his ear. "This sounds like long distance. Who are you talking to?"

"My sister."

"It is long distance, isn't it? How long have you been talking to her?"

"Just a few minutes."

"And did you ask permission?" We glared at each other. "That's what I thought—sneaking in here without permission. Well, that's all for you, mister." He hung up. "Get out of here."

My faced burned with anger at his hanging up on Jill.

He followed me out, complaining to Zinia, but secretly delighting in finding me out. "Guess what our little friend's been doing—phoning all over the country, for all we know. I'd sure hate to be getting your phone bill next month. No telling how much it'll be."

"Is that right, Jimmy?" Zinia asked.

"I just talked a few minutes to my sister."

"You could've at least asked," Fred said.

"Okay. Can I phone my brother and sister?"

"Not now you can't. Besides, it's too expensive. I don't phone my parents as a rule on Christmas, so why should you phone anybody?"

"Because I love my brother and sister, and you don't love anybody but yourself," I countered.

"You smart-aleck," Fred said.

"Children, children," Rachel interrupted with a grin. "Jeff and I'll take Jimmy out for a drive until supper's ready."

I sat in the back seat while Jeff drove. Rachel sat close to him and put her arm around him and lightly touched the hair on the nape of his neck. She made him drive by her old schools and told him stories of when she was growing up.

Jeff was good-natured and smiled a lot. He had a small mustache that really looked good on him. Besides, he was from California. That made me like him too.

We stopped at her old grade school, and each of us sat on a swing and tried to see who could get the highest. I won because they started laughing and couldn't concentrate on pumping higher.

Jeff bailed out of the swing and landed on his feet, then turned to Rachel with an exultant, "Ta da!"

She slowed down and bailed out too. He caught her when she landed, and she slipped into his arms and he kissed her. We drove around some more, and I fell asleep. When I woke up, they were talking. I kept my eyes closed so they wouldn't know I was awake.

"Six months," he said.

"Six months? And then what?"

He laughed. "And then you'd better watch out."

"I'll be ready," she said with a smile. "Do you want to know about our reception?"

"Not particularly," he said. "Let's talk about our wedding night."

"C'mon, Jeff, it doesn't help to talk about that. Besides, there's a lot of other details to work out."

"Okay, tell me about the details."

She went into a lot of boring things about who was going to make the wedding cake and about the invitations. It was so bad that I pretended to wake up. They kept talking and joking and touching.

I was so lonely.

The first school year in Idaho passed slowly, unbroken in its tedium only by a bus trip in April that our school band took to Idaho Falls. It was during that trip that Scott and I pulled off our weirdest prank. It was before we learned moderation and good taste.

"Now?" Scott whispered to me as the band bus droned on and on.

I looked over at Tammy Patterson and her seatmate, Barbara Jones, the most straight-arrow girl in town. They were sitting across the aisle from us.

"Now."

I casually picked up a sack and walked to the rest room in the back of the bus. Once I'd locked the door, I opened the sack and took out a can opener and a can of beef stew. I dumped the beef stew into a bag the bus provided for car sickness, then laid it into the brown bag and went back to my place and hid it under the seat.

"I don't feel so good," Scott said so Tammy and Barbara would hear it.

Tammy leaned over. "I have some car-sickness pills," she said.

Scott nodded his head slowly. "I need something."

Just as he was about to take the pills, he started gagging. I handed Scott an empty car sickness bag. He grabbed it and bent down and made terrible sounds. The girls turned away. While he was bent over, he switched bags. When he sat up, he thrust the bag full of beef stew at me and moaned for me to get rid of it.

I looked curiously at the contents of the bag. "Hmmm," I said.

Tammy stared at me with horror as I picked out a chunk of meat from the beef stew and popped it into my mouth. She ran screaming down the aisle to the rest room. I smiled at Barbara, then picked out another chunk of meat and ate it. Barbara ran away also.

As soon as they left, we threw the beef stew out the window and opened our magazines and innocently started reading.

The girls in the back of the bus were gagging and trying to explain what they'd seen.

"Ohhh! Gross!" Barbara cried out.

Mr. Miller, our band teacher, walked back to see what was wrong. In a few seconds he returned. He reached down and pulled me up by the shoulders and shook me hard.

"Pepper, I oughta throw you off the bus!" he yelled.

"What for?" I asked.

"Tammy says Scott threw up and you ate it."

"It was just a joke, Mr. Miller. It was really beef stew."

"A joke?" he shouted. "What kind of joke is that? You go back and apologize to them right now!"

He stormed away.

I walked back to Tammy and Barbara.

"I'm sorry for pulling that joke on you."

"It wasn't funny, Jimmy."

"I know. I'm sorry. I thought it would be. It's hard to know beforehand."

"That's all you care about, isn't it!" Barbara lashed out. "You don't think about whether something's right or wrong, do you! All you care about is if it's funny or not." She left to get away from me.

I sat down with Tammy. "I'm sorry. I really am. I thought it'd be funny."

She smiled just a little. "Well, it sort of was, I guess, in a way."

"Can I sit with you?"

"Okay," she said, giving me a shy yet warm smile.

Two weeks later we attended a ward potluck supper. It was crowded with a long line. Tammy was there. We started talking in the hall.

"Have you ever kissed a girl?" she asked.

"No," I said.

"Would you like to?"

A few minutes later we sauntered into a classroom for my first kiss while everyone else was going through the line piling tuna and noodles on their paper plates.

It wasn't love. It was a long food line and boredom with potluck suppers and curiosity. Lots of people kiss, but we made the mistake of kissing in a classroom at church during a potluck social. We also had the bad luck to be found out by Sister Mills, a lady who had never been married. She was the ward expert on genealogy. To my fifteen-year-old mind it seemed she loved the dead more than the living.

She opened the door quietly during our second kiss, saw us, and gasped, "What's going on here?"

We broke apart. "Nothing," I said quickly. "The line was so long . . . uhh . . . we were just talking."

"Don't lie! I know what you were doing."

Another lady showed up at the door.

"I caught 'em in here kissing," Sister Mills said. "In a classroom, mind you. Can you believe that?"

The other lady looked at me and nodded. "Jimmy Pepper—I might've guessed. Young man, do you realize this is the Lord's classroom?"

"He wasn't using it," I said like a reflex action triggered by any possibility for a joke, whether or not in good taste.

Sister Mills turned beet red. "I ought to slap your face."

By then several persons stood at the doorway, gaping at us. Tammy started to cry and ran out of the room.

Now there was just me and the crowd.

My Sunday School teacher stood in the hall and looked at me. She was about seventy years old. "Jimmy, why would you want to desecrate our church?"

"I don't have a car," I said.

"What'd he say?" someone on the fringe of the crowd asked.

"He said he doesn't have a car."

"What's that got to do with it?"

"If he did, he'd have parked out on some country road with the girl."

"What's happening to our youth?" a woman said.

"He's not ours, you know. He's one of those foster kids."

"It's a case of one bad apple in the barrel," another observed.

"We've got to do something about it," a woman said.

The next morning at breakfast Logan told me he wanted to talk to me in his shed. As we walked out there, I remember wondering how bad he was going to hurt me. He'd built the shed as a place for his tools. It was a small pole barn with rough wood floors and a large workbench with tools hanging from a white painted plywood panel above the workbench. The outline of each tool was painted in red, so you'd know where to put the tool when you were through with it. Every bolt, every nut and washer was located in baby food jars with lids on them. The jars hung from a homemade lazy Susan, with the size and thread of each item printed on the bottle in Logan's writing. A large radial arm saw was in the middle of the room, and on another wall several shovels hung from clamps. Logan serviced his own vehicles and there was a tool chest on wheels full of wrenches.

This was man's domain. I'd never seen Zinia as much as step inside the shed. No curtains hung from the one window, and no little knickknacks cluttered the workbench.

We walked in and he shut the door. There was no place to sit down. He turned to face me. His face was red—he was as embarrassed as I.

"I don't want you fooling around," he said.

"No sir," I said, wishing I could crawl through the cracks in the floor.

"The things that a man and woman do," he said, clearing his throat, "that's reserved for marriage. Do you understand, or do I have to spell it out?"

I'd have died rather than have him spell it out. "I understand," I said quickly.

"And don't go kissing girls in the church anymore. You know better than that."

"Yes sir."

"All right then. Go get your chores done." He turned and walked quickly out the door.

The bishop set up a way for me and Tammy to repent. He talked to her just one time, but I guess he figured I needed more work. We started meeting once a week. Everybody in the ward knew I was meeting with the bishop. I guess they figured it was awful punishment. Actually it wasn't bad at all. Even at that age I'd figured out that if you were in trouble, the best thing to do was to go talk to your bishop.

It was our third interview. The previous week I'd written a letter of apology to Tammy's parents. He helped me write it.

He said he wanted to know if there were any other things I could work on while we were meeting. He gave me a long interview. We spent a long time on being morally clean, then moved on to other things.

"Tell me what being honest means to you," he said.

"Always telling the truth and not stealing anything."

"Do you always tell the truth?"

I paused before answering. "Not always."

"When don't you tell the truth?"

Long silence. Finally I said, "Well, for instance, this interview."

"Do you want to talk about it, Jimmy?"

"I can't," I said miserably.

"Maybe I can help."

"If I tell, you'll never talk to me again."

"I'll always be your friend, no matter what."

Eventually I decided to talk to him. "You asked if there was anything bothering me and I said no, but there is. Once I had a dream. My sister and I were on a bus, but

instead of going here we were going to California, and
she showed me a letter that said she wasn't really my sister—that there'd been a mistake and they'd mixed babies
in the hospital—and so we weren't really related . . ." I
stopped. My forehead was beaded with sweat.

"Have you told her about your dream?"

"I'll never tell her. She'd think I was weird. If you
knew her, bishop—she's ten times neater than any other
girl. Especially the ones in this ward. No offense, but we
really got some dogs in this ward. People think I care for
Tammy, but I don't, not a fig. That's what Zinia is always
saying—not a fig. Well, it's true. I don't care a fig for
Tammy. It was her idea, you know, to go kiss in the classroom."

The bishop wasn't yelling at me. I decided to keep
talking.

"Jill can swim the length of a regular-size pool under
water. You think Tammy can do that? No sir. I bet there's
not a girl in this town who can do that."

"Probably not." He smiled.

"I miss her, bishop. We don't have a mother or father
anymore. It's just the three of us, but they never let me
see 'em. Jill could help me, I know she could help me.
And Ryan—that's my brother—Jill and I'd help him.
Bishop, he's such a worrywart, and it'd be good for him
to be around me. I'd be a help to him. I'd teach him not to
worry about homework. He worries, you know, about
school. I never do. I could help him."

It all started tumbling out now. "Sometimes, I want to
see her so much—and Ryan too." My voice faded away.

He handed me a tissue. I blew my nose.

"Bishop, what if I never know anyone neater than
Jill? What if all the girls I ever meet are dull and ugly and
dumb compared to Jill? What will I do then? It bothers
me a lot."

"You're afraid your sister is the only girl you'll ever
love? And you know you can't marry her. Is that how you
feel?"

It was a relief just to know he understood. "That's right—that's the way I feel."

"Jimmy, somewhere there's a girl growing up, the one you'll marry in the temple. When you find her, she'll even top your sister."

"You think so?"

"I'm sure of it," he said with a wry grin. "I have a sister too."

I left the interview feeling twenty pounds lighter.

Summer came. At least it meant school was over, but I traded one set of duties for another. My duties involved weeding the family garden and helping Logan farm the place.

Some days he wouldn't say more than a dozen extra words to me even when we were working side by side. He wasn't mad at me, he just wasn't a big talker. But he tried to teach me things. In the middle of a field he'd say, "I need a three-eighths socket head wrench." I'd run to the pickup, open the tool box, and wonder what he wanted. I'd pick up everything that looked like a wrench and bring it all to him. Invariably in the time I took, he would have fixed it another way without the wrench. "I don't need it anymore. Take all that stuff back." And I'd dutifully obey.

Sometimes he seemed so melancholy. I had the feeling he knew the tractor'd break down just when he needed it, and he'd have to order parts, but when the parts finally came, they'd be the wrong parts. He knew it, and when it happened, it only confirmed what he knew—that you can't win and you can't even break even. Maybe it was the look of a farmer, that when your crop is destroyed, the prices are good, but when you have a good crop, the price is below the cost of production.

Duty called loudly and consistently in the Larsen home. It called in the fields. A person worked every day on the farm because duty demanded it. And then on

Saturday night, you put away your tools and implements and went into the house to get ready for going home teaching, then came home and laid out your Sunday clothes and went to bed to arise the next morning for a Sabbath day of duty.

I was the wrong boy for that household, because I hated duty and order and neatness. And it was the first time in my life I'd been asked to do something other than what suited my fancy.

Logan knew I was eating more in food than I'd ever be worth to him on the farm, and yet he kept me. I'm not sure why. In the beginning he never talked about his feelings. Steady as a rock, steady as the fact that every morning in the summer we would beat the sun up and work until past the time it set.

Logan never read much other than the scriptures. But I read every science fiction book they had in the library. I was hoping for aliens to come and rescue me.

That summer I went to Rachel and Jeff's wedding reception. They'd been married a couple of days earlier in the Idaho Falls Temple. They looked so good together, so happy, full of jokes and smiles and hugs and winks. Just watching them was better than any lesson in church about chastity.

I went through the reception line, shaking hands with everybody. When I came to Rachel, she leaned over and kissed me on the cheek. Then she whispered in my ear—so loud that everyone could hear—"It was worth the wait."

The conversation in the reception line stopped.

I went through the line blushing, then left to eat all the pecans, almonds, and Brazil nuts from the nut tray, leaving only the peanuts for everyone else.

CHAPTER FOUR

My second Christmas in Idaho came and with it the gathering of Logan and Zinia's family. This time Rachel was pregnant. Jeff was finishing his senior year at BYU and had taken a job in Los Angeles as a junior executive. He'd start in June. Fred and his wife were also there for the holidays, as well as Ruth and Andrew. Fred was unhappy with his job because he wasn't moving up fast enough. Seeing the way he acted around his family, I figured if he wasn't being demoted, he was rising up as fast as possible.

Fred had a new camera and tripod. He made a big production of assembling everybody together for a family portrait, then asked me to take the picture. He took his place standing in the center with one hand laid on Logan's shoulder.

"We need Jimmy in the picture too, don't we?" Rachel asked.

"We just want the *real* family," Fred said. To me he said, "Take the picture now."

I looked through the lens.

"Don't fiddle with the camera," Fred said. When he was mad, as he was then, he spoke in a slow, crisp style, making him sound especially in control. "I've—already—focused it. Just—push—the shutter."

I tried to find the shutter. There were about a thousand knobs and buttons and settings.

The grandchildren were getting restless.

"I can't find the shutter," I said.

"It's—on the top—there—where the shutter—

should be. Kids, get—back—get in place now. Jimmy's going to take the picture now. Aren't—you—Jimmy?"

One of the grandchildren hit another with a toy shovel. They started crying.

"Just take the picture, will you!" Fred yelled.

I looked at the camera again. There was a button on top.

"Do I have to do everything around here?" Just as he started moving toward me, I pushed the shutter. The flash went off, getting a wonderful picture of his ample stomach.

"What did you do that for?" he snapped.

"You said take the picture," I replied.

"Not when I'm walking toward the camera. Don't you have any sense?"

"Why'd you get a foreign camera anyway? You ever hear of Kodak?"

The grandchildren were scattering through the house.

"You used my last flash!" he complained.

"You said take the picture!"

"You people are all alike, aren't you?" Fred exploded.

"Fred, that's enough," Rachel said.

"What people?" I yelled.

"All my life we had foster kids, breaking my stuff, stealing it too. Poor Homeless Kids, that's all I've heard. Well, what about me? What about Poor Fred! Having to put up with people like you. You people steal things. Don't deny it!"

"Quiet!" Logan demanded.

We became quiet.

"All right, we're through here. Mother, what have you got planned for us?"

"I thought we could all have some nice fruitcake."

Zinia sliced up a fruitcake and got out cookies for the children. We all politely nibbled on our assessed portion of fruitcake.

"It tastes just like last year," Rachel said diplomatically, with only a slight wink in my direction.

"Yes, it's just the way I remember it," Jeff dutifully repeated.

I went outside and threw it into a field and hoped that whatever field mouse ate it wouldn't get too sick.

As a sophomore in high school, I remember spending Friday and Saturday nights, when Scott could get the family car, cruising town, which of course meant driving up and down Main Street, looking for girls. If the girls of America had ever once agreed to stay in one place, there would have been no energy crisis.

This happened on one of those weekends. We were parked at a drive-in having some fries and root beer.

A Corvette drove by.

"Hey, a 'Vette," Scott said.

I looked at it and scowled. "Piece of junk."

"Whataya mean?"

I frowned. "I wouldn't have one if you gave it to me."

"So what's better?"

"A Jaguar XK-E coupe with twin overhead camshafts and four-wheel disc brakes." Of course I'd learned all this from a magazine.

"How much?"

"Six thousand."

He laughed. "You'll never get a Jaguar. Besides, it's not that much better than a 'Vette."

"Whataya talking about? Twin overhead camshaft? You think a 'Vette can top that? You don't know anything."

A car full of girls pulled into the drive-in.

We got out of the car, opened the hood, and leaned over the engine and jiggled wires.

The driver, a girl named Linda, left her car and came toward us.

"Hi, Jimmy." She smiled warmly at me.

"Hey, Linda, how's it going?"

"Hi," Scott said. "What're you doing?"

Nothing. How about you guys?" she said.

I ceremoniously wiped my hands off with a handkerchief. "We were just making a few adjustments."

"On my car," Scott added.

Linda looked at me with admiration. "You understand all about cars, don't you."

Modestly I answered, "Yeah, pretty much everything."

"Both of us do, actually," Scott said.

"It all seems so complicated to me. Can you tell me what the various things are?"

"Oh sure," I beamed.

"And if he makes any mistakes, I'll correct him," Scott said.

"Now this here's the battery," I said. "This particular one happens to be a 12-volt battery. It's very important to know if your car has a 6-volt or a 12-volt battery. Do you know what kind your car has?"

"I always thought a battery was . . . well . . just a battery."

"Oh, gosh no," I said. "There's 12-volt batteries and there's 6-volt batteries. If you were to put a 12-volt battery where it needs a 6-volt battery, it'd wreck your whole car."

"Absolutely ruin it," Scott added.

By this time she was standing close to me, while I pointed to the battery. I could even smell her shampoo.

"Who else is in your car?" Scott asked.

"Well, there's Vicky Colby and Janice Engstrom and, let's see, who else—Carol Smith—and my sister."

Scott went down the list in his head. Just as we would have Jaguars and Corvettes, we were equally discriminating about the girls we'd spend time with at a drive-in on a Friday night. "Do you think your sister would like me to explain about cars?" he asked.

She frowned. "We really need to get home. My parents just sent me out to get a loaf of bread."

They drove away.

"Well, thanks a lot," I grumbled, slamming the hood shut.

"What'd I do?"

"You scared her away, that's what."

"How'd I scare her away?"

"By asking about her sister. She didn't want you with her younger sister. Why didn't you just ask for Carol Smith, for crying out loud?"

"Carol Smith? Are you crazy? You think I'd go out with Carol Smith?"

"They why didn't you just shut up and let me talk to Linda? You realize she leaned into me when I pointed at the battery?"

"What am I supposed to do? Sit and watch you two drool over the battery all night?"

We returned to the car and listened to the radio. The drive-in was momentarily empty.

I hit my fist on the dashboard. "I wonder where everybody is."

"Probably at a party we weren't even invited to," Scott said glumly.

We finally gave up and went to my place to pop some popcorn, and then we went in my room and listened to my radio. He got up to look around. On the dresser was a picture of Jill that she'd sent me a few days before.

He picked it up and looked at it. "This your sister?"

"Yeah."

"Nice."

"Yeah, she's okay."

"Where'd you say she lives?"

"Twin Falls."

He turned around. "Let's go see her."

"Now?"

"Sure."

"It's too late."

"Tomorrow morning then. I can get the car, and I'll pay for the gas."

"What for?"

"Just to see her."

"Okay."

The next morning at ten-thirty we finally pulled up to her address, a white house with a fence near the edge of Twin Falls.

"Is Jill here?" I asked her foster mother. She let us in. The sound of a vacuum cleaner droned on somewhere in the house. Then it stopped, and Jill came running into the living room.

"Jimmy!" she said, throwing her arms around me. It felt good to have her close to me.

"Let me look at you." She stepped back. "Wow, you're becoming a man. Look at those muscles."

"Comes from doing chores," I said, grinning.

"And you must've grown four inches since I saw you last."

I looked at her. "You've grown too—in all the right places."

"Yeah, yeah," she said, laughing it off. But still I could tell she was pleased I'd noticed.

Scott cleared his throat.

"This is my best friend. His name is Scott."

"Hi," he said. "Want to go with us and get a milkshake?"

"Let me finish vacuuming my room first, and I'll be right with you."

The vacuuming took about thirty seconds, but she didn't come out for ten minutes, and when she did, she'd changed her clothes and done something with her hair.

She sat between us as we drove around town. At noon we pulled into a drive-in, and Scott made a big fuss about paying for Jill's order. I'd never seen him behave so strangely. He sounded like an ordinary person. Gone was the belching contest we usually had. He didn't get

catsup all over his fingers when he ate his fries, or pretend he'd cut himself, as he usually did. No catcalls to the
waitress as she left with our order. He didn't even crack
his knuckles.

And Jill was strange too. She agreed with absolutely
everything he said. And talk about smiling—I'd never
seen her grin nonstop. She looked like a store manne-
quin—pleasant, neat, and dumb.

I tried to liven things up. "Hey, Scott, let's tell her
about the time we took the beef stew on the bus trip."

He looked at me like I was crazy.

"Do you like music?" he politely asked Jill.

"Very much. How about you?"

"Oh yes," Scott said. "I like to get up in the morning
and have a song with me the rest of the day."

"I do that too," she said.

"Yeah," I added, "Scott likes the song for the Drano
commercial." I sang part of it.

Scott looked at me like I was a five-year-old.

They ignored me. My own sister was being charmed
by my best friend—it was hard to take. I couldn't decide
how I felt. Was I jealous of him for being able to hustle
my sister? Or, seeing the possible end of my closeness
with him, was I jealous of her? It was a mixed bag.

"That's so true," she said at some stupid thing he said.

I belched as loudly as I could.

They looked at me like I was the village idiot.

"Do you think you'll go on a mission?" she asked him.

"Oh, sure."

"That's not what you tell me," I said.

"That's great," she said to him.

The waitress walked by my side of the car. "Hey,
beauty!" I said, leaning out. "What time do you get off
work?"

"Forget it, junior," she said with a scowl.

Now they were talking about poetry.

"I wrote a poem once," Scott said.

"You?" I sneered. "A poem? What kind of poem did you ever write?"

"I'd like to hear it," she said.

Scott began his poem:

> *I want a love,*
> *A love from above.*
> *A beautiful girl*
> *From heaven above.*
> *My own true love.*

I howled and snorted and guffawed.

"What a lovely poem," Jill said.

"Thank you," Scott said.

Finally we finished our food, and Scott started driving around town. He pulled up to a city park, and we all got out, and they started walking together. He put his hand out, and they held hands and talked about poetry. I sat on the hood of his car and practiced seeing how far I could spit.

From then on, a Saturday trip to Twin Falls was a ritual. To keep me occupied, Jill lined me up with a girl named Becky Storm. I dated her every Saturday for a while. I was always in a rotten mood around Scott and Jill.

One night a few weeks later, after a movie, we were outside Jill's home, the four of us. Jill and Scott were having an extended goodnight kiss, and I'd been telling Becky jokes, trying to make her laugh so loud it'd ruin the mood in the front seat and they'd quit kissing. It didn't work.

"Wow, look how late it is," I said as my next ploy.

"Jill," Becky called out, "I need to go home now."

Jill and Scott broke apart.

"What?" Jill called out absently.

"I need to go home now."

"Oh," she said, still a million miles away. "Okay, Becky—good-bye."

"I need a ride home," she said.

"Oh, sure," Jill purred. "Scott, Becky needs a ride home."

It was like watching molasses run to watch them come back to earth.

"A ride home," he repeated. "I have my car—I'll give her a ride home," he said.

"Hey, you two, wake up!" I complained.

"What time is it?" Jill asked.

"Almost midnight," I said.

"I'd better go in," Jill said.

"Not yet," Scott said. "We'll take Becky home first."

Jill's features were softened, her lips open partially, her face flushed.

"Are we ever going to get out of this place?" I demanded. "Becky needs to go home."

We took her home. When I came back from walking her to the door, Scott and Jill were kissing again. I slapped my hand on the door loudly, and they broke apart. I got in front with them.

"What's all this lovey-dovey junk for?" I asked.

"We're in love," Scott said.

"You're both too young to know what true love is."

"Then you're too young to tell us if it is or isn't," Scott said.

"It isn't."

"I don't even think about anybody else anymore," Scott said.

"Me either," Jill said.

I moaned. "C'mon, give me a break. Take me home. I can't stand listening to this garbage anymore."

He walked her to the door and then started kissing her again. I honked the horn a couple of times. Her foster parents came to the door and made Jill go inside.

When Scott came to the car, he was furious at me.

"What's the big deal?" he shouted at me.

"Nothing! Nothing at all. Just drive."

"No, I want to know. What's bugging you?"

"Well, for one thing, I don't like to see you pawing my sister."

"I wasn't pawing her, for crying out loud."

"Just find someone else to hustle. Leave her alone."

He got in the car and drove fast. We didn't say anything until just before we reached my place.

"Find somebody else," I said, "because in a year or two, Jill and I and my brother are going to California. You'll never see her again. So you're just wasting your time."

He stopped and I got out. He said quietly, "I love her."

"She doesn't love you. The only reason she goes out with you is because you're my friend. I mean, if you weren't my friend, she'd never go out with you."

"You're jealous, aren't you. What's the matter? You wish she'd go steady with you?"

I slammed the car door as hard as I could.

He put the car in gear and roared away.

It was the last time we ever double-dated.

But he kept dating Jill.

In August, just before my junior year began, Ryan called to invite Jill and me to his Eagle court of honor. I got permission from Logan to drive his pickup.

On the way Jill made fun of the pickup and called me Farmer Jim. She was full of details about her and Scott and their plans.

"Why don't you like him anymore?" she asked.

"I like him."

"But you two never do things together anymore."

"We will, we will," I said. There was no way I could explain how I felt, since I wasn't even sure myself. I'd just boxed it all up and refused to deal with it.

That night we went to the court of honor. Ryan, the scout-green sash across his chest full of merit badges, stood proudly as his foster mother pinned the award on and kissed him.

Afterwards there was a party at his foster parent's home, with a few girls there from his ward. They looked at Ryan like he was their hero, and he talked with each of them. It didn't seem to matter to him whether or not they were pretty.

After the party was over, Jill and I stayed the night with Ryan. Jill suggested we all sleep out in the backyard, joking how Ryan as an Eagle scout would save us from the bears and lions. There were enough spare sleeping bags in the house, and by eleven o'clock we were lying side by side looking up at the stars. Ryan pointed out the constellations. That interested Jill, but I was bored.

"Let's go steal a watermelon!" I said. "I saw some in a garden about three houses away. They ought to be ripe by now. We'll be back here again in five minutes. C'mon, whataya say?"

Jill giggled. I knew she'd be with me.

"What for?" Ryan asked.

"Just for the heck of it. We'll break it open and eat it right on the lawn."

"That's the Andersons' garden," he said. "I'm not stealing from them."

"Ah, c'mon, Ryan," Jill said. "They've probably got hundreds. They won't miss just one."

"No, it's not right," he said.

"Sometimes you're a real pain, you know that?" I said.

"What's so great about taking something that doesn't belong to us? If you want a watermelon, we'll walk down to a store and buy one."

"That sounds so exciting," I said sarcastically. "What's the matter with you? Afraid of ruining your precious reputation?"

"I'm not going to steal anything."

I got out of the sleeping bag and put on my jeans and a shirt. "Well, I'm going to get a watermelon for Jill and me." I turned to point my finger at Ryan. "You know the trouble with you? You try too hard. You jump through every hoop people tell you to, and you think that'll wash away the past. You want to know what our past is? You ever see a picture of somebody dying from an overdose of drugs? Well, next time you do, remember the stuff might've been brought in the country by dear old dad."

"How do you know that?" he asked.

"It was in the Cheyenne paper. A friend sent it to me. We're the kids of a crook. And it doesn't matter how many badges you pile on that hairless chest of yours, nothing's going to change that."

"Jimmy, shut up!" Jill said.

"Okay, okay. I'll be back in just a minute," I said. "I'm going to get a watermelon."

"Ah, forget it," she said sourly.

Ryan and Jill talked most of the night, with her trying to undo the damage I'd done.

I woke up early in the morning and watched Jill and Ryan asleep. Realizing I'd driven them both away, I tried to think of a way for us to be united again.

"Hey, wake up, you guys." I shook them to get them to wake up.

"You got a knife?" I asked Ryan.

He fumbled in his pocket and gave me his scout knife. I cut my thumb and gave the knife to Jill.

"Do it—like we did before."

She shook her head. "We're too old for that now," she said.

"Ryan?"

"I feel the same way."

"Okay, but hey, no matter what, we've got to stick together. Okay?"

"Okay," they said.

"And sometime soon, we'll all move out to California and live together as a family again. Okay?"

"Maybe," Jill said.

"Maybe," Ryan echoed.

When I drove Jill home and talked about us moving to California, she turned away and looked out the window and didn't say anything.

Almost a year later, in April of my junior year, Logan and Zinia had troubles. It started with Zinia telling Logan he ought to see a doctor. He always said no, but she kept nagging him. Finally she got an appointment and told him he'd have to pay for it whether or not he went. He went.

That night at supper, Logan said the doctor didn't know anything—that no doctors did, and it was just going to cost a lot of money and no good would come of it. I sat and ate and wondered what they were talking about. Eventually I figured out that his doctor wanted him to see a specialist. He didn't want to go, but Zinia finally just told him he was going.

They went the next Saturday morning, and I stayed home and did chores.

When they came home, they got in a big argument. The doctor said Logan had to have surgery, but Logan didn't want to. Zinia blew up at him and said she wanted him alive, and he'd die unless he had the operation. He said he didn't care, that he'd just as soon be dead as to have to live with that.

Zinia won. I knew she would.

The operation was scheduled two weeks later in Salt Lake City. They didn't tell their kids because of some cockeyed idea about not wanting to have their children worry.

I was the only one in the family who knew. The others were away, so it was easy to keep it a secret. They wouldn't tell me what kind of an operation it was. I asked Logan once, and he shook his head and walked away.

Just before we left to go to Salt Lake City, Logan left me with the job of loading suitcases while he went to his shed. I finished loading the last suitcase, then went to the shed. He was standing there staring at his tools neatly hung from their hooks.

"Anything wrong?" I asked.

He turned around and said quietly, "Just thinking about putting in a cement floor someday."

He walked away.

He didn't fool me. He wasn't thinking about a cement floor. He was thinking he might die and never come back to his farm. But he wouldn't ever let on that he was worried. That's just the way he was.

They'd obtained permission for me to get out of school and go with them. They let me drive most of the way. I kept the radio on, because they were both so quiet and I needed something to keep me awake.

It was strange about Logan and Zinia. When we got to Salt Lake City, they shopped for motels. We'd stop and Logan would walk into the office and ask the price, then shake his head and come back out again and we'd drive to the next one—until finally he found one cheaper than all the rest.

There's a good reason why some motels are so cheap—it's because they *are* cheap. Our room was dark and dingy, with a black and white TV that kept fluttering no matter what you did with the vertical control. The walls were paper thin. The couple next to us had a little baby that cried all night, and if the baby wasn't enough, we had to listen to them argue about why it was crying. The guy kept saying for her to do something about it. Zinia said they ought to put the kid on solids.

I woke up at three in the morning. I was sleeping on a roll-away that stuck out into the room, so it was almost wall-to-wall beds. The baby in the next room was asleep, but I could hear Logan and Zinia talking in low whispers. He was telling her about the stocks and bonds and the will. I looked over and saw him running his finger over the outline of her face.

"Are you my sweet gal?" he asked softly.

"You know that—I'll always be your sweet gal."

"That's right—you're my sweet gal."

I was embarrassed for them because they were so old. I wondered how he could say that to her, because she had wrinkles on her face and her hair was a dull color, and she didn't wear lipstick and never used perfume, and there was just a little bit of mustache beneath her nose, and she had dark plastic glasses that hid her eyes. How could he ask if she was his sweet gal?

I was afraid of hearing anything more, afraid they'd say or do something that'd really embarrass me, thinking I was asleep when I wasn't. They were old people, afraid of death in the morning, their children married and having children themselves—and there they were, old people, him asking if she was his sweet gal.

I couldn't handle it.

I got out of bed and stumbled to the bathroom and made as much noise as I could, flushing the toilet, turning the faucets on and off, brushing my teeth, and even gargling—so they'd know I was awake, and they'd better be careful and not embarrass me. When I returned, they were far apart in bed, facing away from each other at opposite sides.

I was satisfied and went to sleep.

Logan got us up at seven the next morning. After I was dressed, he asked me to help him fold up the rollaway. I told him we could leave it for the maid, but he said it wouldn't kill us to do a little work.

Zinia came out of the bathroom wearing a Sunday dress. Logan brought in from the car a box labeled

"Breakfast." Zinia made up some powdered milk and took out three plastic bowls and spoons and a box of cereal from the box. There were also bananas to have on our cereal.

"This'll be my last meal till after the operation," Logan said.

I thought about that—his last meal maybe in his life. I knew what I'd have done. I'd have gone to a pancake restaurant and had the biggest breakfast on the menu. There's no way I'd bring food from home to eat in a dingy room in the cheapest motel on State Street. But not Logan and Zinia. I figured if she'd been in charge of the Last Supper, they'd have had macaroni and cheese and carrot sticks.

After breakfast we drove to the hospital and Logan checked in. The doctors had to do some tests, and they said Zinia might as well leave the hospital until the afternoon, when she'd be able to see Logan, but she said no, she'd just stay and wait.

We sat in the waiting room and pretended to read magazines. She'd brought some knitting with her so she wouldn't waste time. She was strange that way. I could waste time and never give it a thought, but it made her feel guilty, and so she knitted.

I read all the women's magazines I could stomach. You just don't find *Sports Illustrated* in a hospital waiting room, but there were plenty of *Redbook* and the like. I'd read all the articles that had to do with marriage relationships, and pretty soon they all took on the same pattern. The article would first talk about a problem—any problem, you name it—and then they'd say the problem was only symptomatic of a more serious problem called lack of communication. I decided you could go a long way as a marriage counselor if, no matter what problems people brought, you just said it was a lack of communication.

It was 1973, and I was seventeen. The Vietnam War was over for the United States, but the news magazines in the waiting room dated back quite a ways. They had articles about Vietnam, showing bodies spattered with blood lying on the ground. I wondered if I'd get drafted for some unknown war and end up dead with someone taking a picture of my body for a magazine. Maybe I'd be dead before I had a chance to get married or own a Jaguar.

I decided to go back to the women's magazines.

Finally I got tired of reading. I asked if I could walk around the hospital. Zinia said yes but I was not to get into any trouble. I said I wouldn't.

I walked down the long halls and peeked in each room to see what was happening. In one room an old man was moaning with pain, crying out over and over, "Oh, my leg, my leg." I stopped and looked in. His face was contorted with pain. I watched him for a long time. When I started out again, there was a slight pain in my leg, and I wondered if what he had was contagious. I prayed I wouldn't get it but then felt guilty for only thinking of myself. So I prayed the old man would either get better soon or die.

I moved on. The walkers were out—patients in crumpled white gowns, leaning on aluminum walkers with nurses' aides at their sides. On the maternity floor (a floor I wasn't supposed to be on) young mothers took tender steps down the hall, talking about sitz baths and husbands and weights of babies.

I decided it was pretty much the same with people as it is with animals: if their coat has a nice shine to it, they're healthy. The patients with their hair looking the worst were the sickest.

Zinia and I stayed the night in the same motel. The next morning we got up at four and drove to the hospital. We arrived early enough to go with Logan when he was wheeled to the operating room. After the operation started, we went to the waiting room. Zinia gave me money to eat breakfast in the hospital cafeteria. She said she wasn't hungry.

I ate, then went back. She was sitting there, staring at

the endless patterns of tiles down the hall. She looked worried.

"What's wrong with Logan?" I asked.

"It's a tumor," she said.

"What are they going to do with it?"

"Remove it."

"That doesn't sound so bad."

"It might be malignant," she said.

"What does that mean?"

"Cancer," she said with difficulty.

I raised my eyebrows. "Logan has cancer?"

"We don't know. We'll know in a while."

Instead of making my rounds through the halls as I'd planned, I sat with her. She needed me.

Four hours later, the doctor came out to see us. He sat down and talked calmly about the operation. He said the tumor had been malignant, but it had been localized, and they'd removed it. They'd performed a colostomy. He said he was sure Logan could adapt to it. There were thousands of people in the country who'd had the same operation and adjusted very well. He said there was a lady who dealt with colostomy patients and their families, and he gave us her office number and said if we'd go there, she'd explain things more completely.

Zinia thanked him, and he left us. She sat and watched him leave. There were tears in her eyes. I didn't know what to say. She finally got up and started walking away. She forgot her knitting. I gathered it all in her bag and carried it with me.

The colostomy lady was waiting for us. She took us into another room, where there was a plastic model of a person's insides, with red and blue and green parts that could be taken apart. She explained the operation to us very carefully. For a while I didn't understand what she was saying, but then I finally did.

* * * * * * * * * * * * *

A few days later they released Logan from the hospital and we drove home. Logan was more withdrawn and quieter than usual. When we got home, he went to bed.

They woke me the next morning shouting at each other, or at least Logan was yelling at her. They were both in the bathroom, and the door was closed.

"Just leave me alone," Logan grumbled.

"I want to help," she said.

"I don't want any help! Can't you get it through that thick head of yours? Now just get out of here and leave me alone. Oh, I wish I was dead."

"Well, I don't. No sir, I don't wish that at all."

"Spending my whole life doing this . . . it's gonna take hours—and be a mess."

"No it won't, Logan. Please let me help you."

He blew up. "Get out of here!"

Silence.

His voice was strange. "I don't want you to see me this way. Can't you get that in your head? Now get out."

She came out crying. Logan locked the door after she left. She breezed past my bedroom door to their room.

A few minutes of silence, then sounds of choking and groaning from the bathroom.

Zinia ran to the bathroom door and cried out, "Let me in!"

"Stay away!"

"What happened?"

"It's made me sick, and I threw up."

"Let me clean it up."

"How many times do I have to tell you? I don't want you to see what I've become."

"You think I care about a little mess? Why, land sakes, Logan, I've been cleaning up messes all my life. Now you let me in, or I'm getting Jimmy and he'll figure out a way to break in."

The door opened.

"Take a look," Logan said miserably. "It's all over everything."

"Doesn't matter a bit. This bathroom's seen a lot worse than that. Now you leave this door open while I go get a bucket and a rag."

She returned in a minute with a bucket. I got out of bed and walked quietly to the bathroom and peered in. They didn't notice me. He was standing there, watching, while she, on her hands and knees, vigorously attacked the mess. I saw a plastic tube coming out his side.

"I'm more trouble than I'm worth."

"This doesn't matter," she said. "Doesn't matter at all."

"Aw, Zinia," he moaned.

She looked up. "Logan, I'd clean this up ten times a day just to have you with me. You know I would. So don't fret yourself about it, not at all. You hear me? Not at all."

"Zinia, you're my sweet gal." He reached out and touched her head lightly. She paused, delighted in his touch. Then slowly he removed his hand and she went back to work.

I tiptoed back to my room. It was good for me to know that no matter what, they wouldn't run out on each other when things got tough.

After Logan got home, he asked me to do the farm work he normally did. Every day he'd give me instructions about what to do, and I'd go out to work by myself, trying the best I could to do a good job for him. By then I loved them both and just wanted to make them happy with me. The silent anger had been stilled for a time.

I wanted to be their son.

Sometimes Logan would come out to see me in the fields and look over what I'd done and tell me what was wrong with it. He wasn't all the time dishing out praise, but when he gave it, you knew you'd done a good job, and that he wasn't just being polite.

One day in August he came to the fields. It was a

warm day. He sat in his pickup and watched me work. By this time I knew what to do.

When I was through with that job, he called me over.

"Finish up. We're going camping."

I didn't know that Logan even knew what camping was. It wasn't exactly roughing it. Logan had borrowed a neighbor's camper, so we had beds and a small refrigerator and a stove. We packed some provisions and took off. A few hours later we were in the mountains, beside a mountain stream. We tried fishing but didn't catch anything, but it didn't matter, it was fun anyway. Then we made a campfire and cooked some steaks he'd brought in a cooler. After dark, we sat around and talked.

"You saved my crops this summer," he said. "If it hadn't been for you, I'd have lost it all. My farm is my life, you know." His face clouded. "My kids are all too good for it. Somehow they think they're too good to get down and get a little dirt on 'em. College graduates, too good to farm. So what'll happen to this place after I'm gone? There's nobody in the family to carry on here."

"I can, Logan. I know how."

He put his arm on my shoulder. "Yeah, you could. You know most of what I know now. We'll have to think about that, won't we. Some day soon."

He stared somberly into the glowing ashes.

"The tumor they took out—it had cancer in it."

"But they got it, Logan. I heard the doctor say."

"How could they get it all? What if they just missed one cell? You know how small a cell is? One cell, that's all it takes. One cell to go someplace else and start up again. How can they know if they got it all? It'll come back someday."

"Maybe not," I said.

"Do you ever think about dying?"

I shook my head.

"No, of course you don't. I never did either when I

was your age. Even in the war, I never thought it'd happen to me. I bet the ones that died thought the same thing. How else could anybody go to war?"

"Where were you in the war?"

"Pacific."

"What was it like?"

"Bad."

I figured that'd be my lesson about the Second World War, but he continued.

"Once we were in Hawaii to rest up after we'd fought to take some islands. We camped on the side of a mountain. It was very green because it rained so much, and the winds came across the mountain all the time. The fighting had been so bad. And we all knew we had to go back. A fella tried to kill himself by jumping off the mountain, but the wind was blowing so much it pinned him against the side of the cliff and he just slid down to the ground. All that happened was he sprained his ankle. I never found out what happened to him after that, but I always wondered if it was like getting another chance at life. Well, it's late. We'd better get some sleep."

The next morning we returned home. He never told me why he'd taken me with him, but I sensed it was to tell me he loved me.

Just before school started, when I came in from chores one day, Logan asked me to go outside with him. I thought he'd be chewing on me for forgetting to do something.

We walked out to where the cars were kept. There was an extra car there, a Mercury.

"Like it?" he asked.

"Sure, why?"

"It's yours."

I shouted and giggled and laughed and almost cried.

My first car. It wasn't just a car, it was a trust. It was saying that I'd done a good job for him, that I was worth something to them. It was love and trust and reward for working.

Logan loved me.

My senior year of high school started out to be the best time but ended up the worst. I settled down in church, became more mature, less of a clown in classes. The bishop asked me to prepare for a mission soon, and Logan and Zinia said they'd support me.

Logan had by then adjusted to slowing down. He and Zinia even had their children home for Christmas, with none of them suspecting anything.

Just before school started, Ryan invited me to go with him to a youth conference held in his stake. We roomed together during the conference, which was held at a college. The amazing thing to me was how much Ryan was liked and respected, even though he was only fifteen.

Earlier that night, before the dance, there were separate meetings for the boys and girls. We went and heard a very serious talk by the stake president about standards. It was one of those talks you try hard not to blush at.

As we got ready for bed that night, I said, "Ryan, you're really something."

"No I'm not."

"Everyone loves you. All I have to do is tell people I'm your brother and they just flip. You've charmed everybody. Ryan Pepper, Eagle Scout; Ryan Pepper, ace student, winner of ninth-grade class officer election; Ryan Pepper, star seminary student, winner of all the scripture chases. What's your secret?"

"What do you mean?" he asked, suddenly on the defensive.

I looked at his expression and could tell he was hiding something. "Is something wrong?"

"I'm not as good as people think," he said.

"Well, it can't be too bad."

"Why can't it?" he snapped.

"Because anyone looking at you can tell you're good. If it were too bad, it'd show. So what's your big problem?"

"I can't tell you. I can't tell anyone."

I sat down on the bed. "Hey, you can't carry something like that alone. Look, take it from a pro—go talk to your bishop. It really helps."

"I can't."

"Why not?"

"I can't tell anyone."

"He'll help you."

"How do you know? You don't even know what my problem is."

"That's right, I don't. But go talk to him—please."

"I'll wait till I've got it under control."

"That's dumb. Sometimes you need help. Everybody does. That's what he's there for, to help people."

"I shouldn't even have this problem. I should be above it."

"But you're not. What's wrong? Afraid to admit you're not perfect?"

Tears filled his eyes. "I can't tell him."

"I know it's tough, but he'll help."

His bishop was one of the chaperons. I knocked on his door and told him Ryan needed to talk. It was one o'clock.

I waited in the hall while they talked. I could hear Ryan crying.

Thirty minutes went by.

The bishop came out with his arm around Ryan's shoulder, telling him he'd work with him. Then he shook my hand and thanked me for talking Ryan into seeing him.

"It's going to be all right now," the bishop said, then left.

Ryan looked sheepishly at me. "You won't tell Jill, will you?"

"No, of course not."

"I want to be good, but lately it's been like I've lost control."

"Hey, look, don't worry about it. Besides, you're the best there is."

"That's what everybody says, but lately whenever they say it, I think if they really knew what I was like, they wouldn't even talk to me. Maybe you're right, maybe I try too hard. Maybe I've got too much of Dad in me."

"No, you're more like Mom. She was good and so are you."

"You think so, even now?"

"Absolutely. Don't worry about it. You're not like Dad at all."

There were tears in his eyes. My little brother, my Gold Star good-guy brother.

"I want to go on a mission. Do you?"

I paused. "I'm not sure."

"Don't you have a testimony?"

"I don't know. Everytime I go to class, instead of listening to the teacher, I spend all my time thinking of jokes."

"You ought to listen."

I yawned. "I guess so. Can we go to sleep now?"

After that I think he was embarrassed that I knew he had a problem once. But actually I guess it made me love him more to know he was human and had to repent like everyone else.

In January of my senior year, Logan began to limp. He said he had a charley horse, but it never went away. By April the pain was bad enough for him to go to a doctor. Nothing the doctor did made things any better. Finally he was admitted to the hospital in Salt Lake City.

High school graduation came the last of May. I remember listening to the commencement speaker tell us enthusiastically this was really the beginning, not the end.

Zinia called the family and asked them to visit their father while they still could. Over the next few weeks they came, entering his room and lying about how good he looked and how he'd be up in no time. And then they'd come out in the living room and cry.

He died quietly in the night near the end of June.

The night before the funeral there was a viewing of the body at the mortuary. At first just the family was there. I looked in the coffin. Logan looked awful, not because he was dead, but because the funeral director had put makeup on him that made his face look pink and chalky. He was dressed in white clothes. Zinia told me that it had something to do with temples and the resurrection.

I looked at him and imagined a graveyard and him popping out one day, looking around, and walking down the road to his place to see how the potatoes were doing. He'd always want to know that, resurrected or not.

The others in the family took their turns staring into the coffin. Some of them remarked how nice he looked. He didn't look nice to me. To me he looked dead.

Rachel hugged me. I started crying, and she said it was all right. I told her I loved Logan, and she said she knew it, and I'd always be part of the family. Jeff hugged me too. They took me outside, and we walked around the garden. I told them how hard I'd worked the previous summer when Logan was recovering from his operation, and how he gave me a car.

When we went back in, there were a lot of people milling around and talking. They ignored him, like he was the centerpiece on a table at a Shaklee convention.

Fred was talking about being laid off in his job, and how nobody did anything right where he used to work, how he was the only one who knew how things should go, and how sorry they'd be someday for firing him.

The next day we gathered in a room at church just before the funeral started. When it was time to go into the chapel, Fred announced that, since he was the oldest, he and his wife Margaret would sit on either side of Zinia, with Ruth and Andrew next to them.

"What about the grandchildren?" Ruth asked.

"I think there'll be room for my Todd and Howard to sit on the first row. The other grandchildren will have to sit on the second row."

"I think it's better if the parents sit with their children," Rachel suggested.

"All right—Margaret and I will sit beside Mom with our kids on the first row, and the rest of you can sit on the second row. Is that all right with everyone?"

"I want to sit near Mom too," Ruth said. "I'm Logan's child too, you know."

Fred scowled. "There's just not room for everyone on the first row. You're delaying the service, Ruth, and frankly, I'm surprised at your attitude. At a time like this I'd hope you wouldn't be so childish as to worry about where you sit. C'mon, Mom, you come with me."

We formed a line. I was the last one.

The speakers said nice things about Logan during the funeral, and as nice as the words were, they weren't as good as they could have been. Logan was the best man I've ever known. I still hear his voice telling me things. I don't always listen, but I still hear it.

After the funeral we went to the cemetery for a graveside service. Fred said a little prayer over the grave, asking that the ground be kept undisturbed until the resurrection. Then we went back to the house. The women from the church had brought in food for the family, and the table was loaded with salads and casseroles and hot rolls and cakes and pies. It was the best meal I'd seen in that house.

I didn't like the way everybody was eating, like it was some big holiday. Fred packed away two big helpings of food, and Ruth—you should see her eat sometime.

Afterwards we all went into the living room. Fred stood up like he was master of ceremonies.

"I don't know if anybody's thought about it," Ruth said, "but I'd like his collection of silver dollars, if that's all right with everyone."

"Oh sure," Rachel said.

"Exactly why do you want it?" Fred asked.

"What do you mean, why?"

"Is it because you like the collection or because you know what it's worth?"

"I resent that, Fred," Andrew said.

Fred took a mint from a candy dish. "All I'm saying is it'd be nice to know how much it's worth. The reasonable thing would be to find out the cost and then decide if Ruth should have it, or if we should sell it and split the money among the children."

"I'd like his tools," Andrew asked.

Zinia sat there, still in shock. Fred was running the show. He continued. "We'll talk about the silver dollar collection and the tools later. Right now, I'd like to present a little plan I've worked on for the property. Mom can't work the farm, and none of us is really that interested in farming, so I was thinking about turning some of the land into a housing development."

I sat there, consigned to the outer fringes with all the little kids. Suddenly tears started down my face. I got up and quietly walked outside. There was work needing to be done, and all I wanted was for everyone to leave so I could go back to doing Logan's chores until the resurrection when he'd come walking toward me in the fields dressed in white, telling me I'd missed a row.

I went in the shed and shut the door. The smell of sawdust and motor oil filled the room. Everything was there just the way he'd left it, the nuts and bolts and washers labeled in their baby food jars, waiting for someone to walk in looking for a 6-32 bolt. I stood in front of the radial arm saw. There was just a speck of sawdust on the floor that'd slipped into the cracks when he was last sawing.

I picked up his irrigating shovel and started crying and couldn't stop. There was a strange voice making desolate, awful moans, and it was my voice. My tears fell on the table of the saw and I worried it'd rust, so I took out my handkerchief and wiped over the surface. But I was still crying while I wiped, so it never got dry.

I stayed there for a long time. When I returned to the living room, Zinia reached out and hugged me before I sat down. Fred was still running the show, going over his plans. I figure he must have been planning this for a long time.

Now, years later, I can see that Fred was just doing what he thought was best. And probably it was. But to me then, he was wrong because he wanted to change Logan's farm.

Fred was still talking. "Okay, that's our best ball-park figure if we decide to develop the land. I'll move back here and manage things to make sure we get the best deals. Now if I'm going to be working full time on this, I'll need to get an extra share of income. That'd only be fair."

"I don't like the idea of taking the land Dad loved and turning it into a housing development," Rachel said.

Fred scowled. "Do you and Jeff want to move out here and learn to grow potatoes?"

"No, but if we sell the land, why not sell it as farmland?"

Fred shook his head. "We could, but there's no money in that. I don't know about you, but my kids need something to get 'em through college. I think we all need that. We'll save the house for Mom, and a little land for her garden, so she won't be out anything, and she'll have a steady income the rest of her life. Mom, I'm really just trying to look out for you."

"I know, dear," Zinia said quietly.

"I think it's a good idea," Ruth said.

"Well, let's vote then. The only ones who are eligible to vote are me and Ruth and Rachel."

"What about Mom?" Rachel asked. "Doesn't she get a vote?"

"That goes without saying, Rachel. Mom, you vote too."

"It sounds so complicated. The rest of you decide what's right and I'll go along with it," she said.

"All in favor raise your hand."

Ruth and Fred raised their hands.

"All opposed."

Rachel raised her hand.

"The motion carries."

Ruth started up again. "Now can we talk about the silver dollar collection?"

"And the tools," Andrew said.

I ran into the fields and stayed there until night, when I thought they'd all be asleep.

When I came in the house, it was late. Fred was sitting at the kitchen table, poring over pages of calculations strung over the table.

"Where's Zinia?"

"Don't bother her. She's gone to bed. There's nothing you can say now that'd be any help."

"I've got to tell her not to sell the land. Logan doesn't want her to."

"How do you know that?"

"He talked to me about it once."

"Well, you can't talk to her now. She took a sleeping pill. I'll tell her, though, first thing in the morning."

"Where's Rachel?"

"She and Jeff've gone to bed."

"Where?"

"In your room. Don't disturb them. Besides, I need to talk to you. Sit down."

I sat down.

"Dad said good things about you. I think you were very important to him, almost like a son."

I am a son, I thought.

"I guess you realize over the years you've received a lot from my parents. A high school education, a car, clothes, books, food—it all adds up."

He wrote down a number.

"Did he ever tell you the story about the man he knew in World War Two who jumped off a mountain?" I said.

He looked at me strangely. "No, he never did."

"I didn't think he would. He told me though."

"It's all in the past, Jimmy. Time marches on. There has to be progress. I'm in charge now, and a lot of things are going to change. My family'll be moving in this house for a while, until we build our own. We'll be turning the land into a subdivision. This won't be a farm anymore."

"Logan doesn't want that to happen," I said.

He kept punching the buttons on his calculator, looking at the numbers flashing on the screen. I felt sorry for Logan. He must have been disappointed in Fred.

Fred cleared his throat and looked at me for the first time. "I just need to know when you'll be leaving, so we can make plans about using your room."

"Logan said he'd send me on a mission and to college and that I could farm the place someday."

Fred looked at me coldly. "I don't suppose you got that in writing, did you?"

I shook my head.

"I didn't think so. Look, I'm sorry. If you were part of the family, it'd be different, but—and I know this may seem harsh—but you're not, regardless of what he may have said. He was getting old, you know, and sometimes when we get old, our judgment isn't always the best. I'm sure you understand, don't you?"

I stood up to leave, numbly walked a few steps, then turned around. "Logan was in Hawaii, back from fighting, and this guy climbed a mountain to kill himself, but the winds stopped him and slammed him against the rocks, and he slid down the side of the cliff, and it didn't kill him."

Fred didn't bother to look up from his calculator. "Right."

I went to my room. Rachel and Jeff were asleep in my bed. As quietly as I could, I started to pack my clothes into a box.

Rachel woke up.

"Jimmy?" she said quietly.

"Yeah."

"What are you doing?"

"Packing."

"Why?"

"Fred said I had to leave."

She got out of bed and put on a robe. "We'll see about this."

She walked into the kitchen. Fred was still punching numbers.

"What on earth do you think you're doing, telling Jimmy to leave? He's a part of us. Dad loved him. I won't stand for it, Fred."

"Hasn't he bled enough from us already? It's about time he got out on his own instead of freeloading from us all the time."

"Mom loves Jimmy as much as I do. She won't have you telling him he has to leave."

"Mom said she'd go along with anything I decide to do."

"Not this she won't, and you know it, Fred."

I was standing at the edge of the kitchen watching them.

One of Rachel's kids started crying. She turned to me.

"We'll work something out. Let me go take care of my baby, then I'll be right back." She left.

Fred scowled at me. "You think you're gonna just keep sponging off us, don't you. Why don't you grow up and quit being such a leach? I've got an idea. Why don't you go to Mexico and get your dad out of jail and help him smuggle drugs?"

I ran to the shed, took down Logan's shovel from the wall, put it in my car, and drove away.

I drove to American Falls to talk to Ryan. It was a little after one in the morning when I arrived. I knew where his bedroom was, so I drove on the lawn under his window, then got out and stood on top of the car and called through the screen until I woke him up. He came outside, wearing just a pair of jeans and no shirt.

"Get packed—we're going to California tonight. Logan's dead, and I just got kicked out of the house."

He sleepily scratched his head. "You want to leave?"

"Yeah, hurry, we'll pick Jill up on our way."

"Does she know?"

"Not yet. C'mon, hurry."

He yawned. "What'll we do in California?"

"We'll live there. C'mon, we promised each other—remember. You have to come with us."

"I need to finish high school first."

"They've got high schools in California."

He looked at me for a long time, then said, "I can't leave my foster family."

"Why not?"

"I just can't, that's all."

"We all promised that if one of us had to leave, the other two would go with him."

"I need to stay and prepare for my mission. My foster family says they'll help send me."

"They're just saying that. When it comes down to it, they won't help you."

"Yes, they will. Going on a mission is very important to me."

"You think you're so blasted perfect and pure, don't you. Well, you're not, you know."

"I never said I was."

With a mocking tone in my voice, I asked, "Do you still have that problem you used to have?"

"No," he said quietly, "it's all cleared up."

I looked at his eyes and could tell there was nothing he was ashamed about. It scared me.

"Jill won't go to California with you," he said.

"Sure she will. We're as close as a brother and sister can be. Ryan, please go with us."

He sighed. "I can't. I need to stay here."

"You're no brother of mine," I snapped, jumping in the car and driving away.

I arrived at Jill's house about three in the morning. I slept in the car until seven, then rang the bell until her foster father came to the door. "What do you want?" he asked.

"I need to talk to Jill."

"She's sleeping."

"I've got to talk to her."

Jill appeared at the door and said it'd be okay, that we'd just talk quietly in the living room.

She sat down. She was wearing a long pale-blue robe. I told her about Fred, then said, "We're going to California today, just like we always planned. I'll take care of you. Honest I will."

She frowned. "Have you talked to Ryan about it?"

I didn't want to tell her about Ryan.

"We'll go get him after we leave. C'mon, Jillsy. It's what we've always dreamed about, the three of us together, a family again."

She paused. "Scott wouldn't want me to leave him."

"There's plenty of guys in California. Besides, if it's really love, it'll stand the test of time."

"We don't have any money."

"I'll get a job. And I'll put you through school, better schools than they got here, believe me. UCLA or Berkeley."

"My foster parents need me to help out with the twins."

"You're just full of excuses, aren't you. How about considering your family for once?"

She looked at a family picture on the mantel taken the previous summer. She was in the picture. She turned to face me. "This is my family too."

"No! Not them! I'm your family—me and Ryan. I'll take care of you."

She turned on me. "I don't want to be taken care of. Why should I run away from here to go to California with you?"

"Is it too much to expect a little family loyalty once in a while?"

"You call it family, and then you twist it till there's no room for anything else. I can't stand it. You have no right to make me feel guilty for falling in love with Scott. You keep wanting me to choose between him and some weird idea of yours about us as a family. Well, it's not right. Sometimes you just smother me. There's no way I'd ever go to California with you. No way in the world."

I stood up. "Okay then, fine, if that's the way you want it. I've had it up to here with this family."

I left. She followed after me.

Her foster mother, said, "Jill, you can't go outside in just your robe."

But she did.

I got in the car and paused to look at her one last time. I knew I was at a crossroads—that if I'd get out of the car and talk it out, my life would go one way, with the church part of it, but if I drove away and lived without the church, there would be other paths to follow.

For an instant time froze. I looked at Jill as if through a microscope, noticing her eyes and the texture of her face.

Her foster mother stood at the front screen door, watching us. Ten steps between Jill and me. Just ten steps. I couldn't cross that distance. Everyone had a home and family but me.

I started the car.

"Jimmy! Don't go!" she called out as I drove away.

I left her with a breeze moving her robe gently around her feet and the early morning sun on her hair.

"Morning, Ace," the army recruiter in San Francisco said six weeks later. "Want some coffee?"

"Why not?" I said.

He poured me a cup. I took a sip. It tasted strange and bitter, and I wondered why anyone drank it. I'd get used to it. There was no reason now to hold back. I'd be just like everybody else—just like my father.

"I'm out of work, and I need a job."

"What do you do?"

I paused. "I'm a comedian."

"Sit down. Fill out this form. The army's full of comedians."

I sat down and started writing.

It was three months since I'd graduated from high school. The commencement speaker had been wrong.

It was not the beginning.

It was the end.

CHAPTER FIVE

We left from Jill's home in Burley at nine at night and traveled as far as West Yellowstone. The next morning while I packed my suitcase, she came to my room and said a man was sitting in a car watching us. As we walked out the door, he took our picture.

I walked over to him. "What's this all about?"

"Alan Becker, 'The National Inquirer.'"

"She's my sister," I said, realizing what they might do with a picture of me coming out of a motel with someone other than my wife.

He grinned. "I know. Hi there, Jill. How's it going, huh? Is it true your brother calls you Jillsy?"

"Listen to me. I don't want my sister's picture in the 'National Inquirer'."

"Hey, don't worry. I take a lot of pictures on an assignment. Most of 'em I don't use. Let's all just stay cool, okay? I'll be with you for the next few days. Where are we going?"

"None of your business."

"Our readers want to know, and I do too. And I'd like a little information about your family. You were raised by foster parents in Idaho. Why was that? What happened to your parents?"

I hurried to our rooms, tossed our suitcases in the car, and roared away.

He followed us. Once I thought I'd lost him by pulling off the main road and stopping. But when we stopped at Old Faithful for breakfast, he came to our table.

"Sure are a lot of tourists on the road this time of year, huh? Amazing how much a bear can slow down traffic. Say, I notice you aren't taking many pictures of your trip. I'll be happy to

*share some of mine. I got a nice one of the two of you at the Paint
Pots. Took it with a telephoto lens. Should turn out great."*
   "Leave us alone!"
   *"Hey, I understand. Just tell me a few things and then I'll
quit bothering you. My partner stayed behind in Idaho. He says
the rumor in high school was that your dad spent time in a Mexi-
can prison for running drugs. Any truth to that?"*
   "Let's go," I said to Jill.
   We left. He ran to his car to follow us.
   *"We've got to ditch him before we get to Buffalo," I said,
careening around a curve, nearly colliding with a bear.*

I spent two years in the Army. That's where I developed a drinking problem. After the Army, I returned
to California and tried to be a comedian. At first the only
steady job I could find was being a clown on weekends at
grocery stores, giving away samples of Mity Fine orange
juice. But things opened up a little at a time. Before long,
I could afford to live in a nice apartment and drive a car
that was only two years old.
   One rainy night in 1978, Jill phoned. It was just a few
months after she'd married Scott in the Idaho Falls Temple. When I heard her voice I knew something was
wrong. "There's been an accident. Ryan's been hurt bad.
He and his missionary companion were riding their bicycles. Ryan was hit by a car."
   "How bad?"
   She paused. "He's dead. I'm going to bring him
home." She started crying. "Jimmy, I can't go through
this alone. Will you go with me?"
   Ryan was dead. The best of the three of us, and he
was gone. It didn't make any sense.
   MasterCard had made the mistake of giving me a
credit card. I drove to the airport and bought a ticket for
Italy.
   A plane schedule mix-up forced us to fly separately.

When I saw Jill at the terminal in Italy, I was again amazed how beautiful she is. We hugged each other and she started to cry. I wanted to say something but didn't know what, so I asked about her flight. She said it was fine. I said my flight was fine too. I asked about Scott. She said he was fine. Everything's fine, I thought miserably.

The mission president and his wife met us once we cleared customs. Their last name was Stone. We spent the rest of the day finishing our preparations, then had supper with President and Sister Stone.

After supper, Jill and I took a walk. To some we may have looked like a strangely somber married couple. The fresh ocean breeze, the white sands, the blue of the Mediterranean, the sparkling homes, the music from sidewalk cafes, the steady stream of American tourists in their gaudy shorts and halter tops and cameras and com-plaining children—it all seemed out of place in our grief.

After a long silence, she said, "He passed his test."

"Sure." I said it quickly so it'd sound like I bought it.

"You don't believe that, do you."

"Why pretend it's part of some grand plan? Ryan wasn't watching where he was going and he ran into a car. What kind of plan is that?"

"You're quite the cynic now, aren't you."

"I call it being realistic."

"And where does religion fit in your realism?"

"You tell me what kind of god raises up a guy like Ryan—good as they come, solid as a rock, not a bad thought in him—then sends him overseas to be bumped off by an Italian driver. Tell me what kind of god would come up with a plan like that."

"Things will work out for Ryan."

"Sure," I said sarcastically. "They've worked out real swell so far, haven't they?"

She let me have it. "What's wrong with you? It's bad enough losing one brother, but now I have to see how messed up you are."

We stopped at a small sidewalk cafe. I ordered a drink. She had nothing.

I took a sip. "Want any? It's very good. It'd be a cultural experience."

"No thanks."

"I won't tell anyone," I taunted.

She looked sadly at me, then shook her head.

"Suit yourself." I took a sip. "Ahh," I sighed.

"Why are you destroying yourself?"

I looked at the glass. "This? It's nothing. I can stop anytime."

"Then why don't you?"

A photographer came and asked if we were on our honeymoon. To avoid saying we came to collect our dead brother's body, I nodded my head. He asked if he could take our picture for a buck. I nodded my head and he stepped back and coaxed us to smile. We didn't. He made a wisecrack about honeymoons.

"Take the stupid picture and get out of here," I muttered. Thirty seconds later he gave me the picture. It was awful. I paid him. He left, no doubt wondering if the marriage would last the weekend.

Jill finally broke our icy silence. "Are you still going with Rebecca or whatever her name is?"

"Not anymore."

"What happened?"

"You don't really care."

"I asked, didn't I?"

"All right, I'll tell you. In the beginning we were really close. But as time passed, a gap developed in our relationship. So we sat down like mature adults and discussed it."

"And what happened from your discussion?"

I sighed. "She left me for a jockey—a small guy, maybe four feet tall. I saw her last week in a grocery store. She said he augments her identity."

"What does that mean?"

"It means she likes being taller than him. It's like Snow White and one dwarf."

She didn't smile. "I assume you and your crowd just reshuffle and deal again."

I ordered another drink. Jill frowned at me. "Do you really need that?"

"Jill, I know what you're gonna say, so don't say it."

"What am I going to say?"

I stared grimly into my glass. "That I should shape up for Ryan's sake."

She touched my arm. "That's not it. Do it for your own sake. What you're doing only brings unhappiness."

I laughed. "Wrong, Jillsy. I'm happy—terrific at parties. Ask anyone in Southern California."

"Jimmy," she pleaded, "please—for my sake then, straighten up your life."

I looked at her. My little sister still loved me. And I loved her. I'd do just about anything for her.

Except change. I shook my head. "Just quit? Now? That'd be real difficult. Sometimes I get lonely, or nervous, or scared, and a drink . . . a drink makes things better."

"If you turn your life around, Heavenly Father will help you find a wife. He's got someone picked out, and He's just waiting for you to get your act together so He can introduce you without having you pass out on the first date."

"That's not kind. I hold my liquor very well."

"Ryan'll help you. I'm sure he will. He always tried to be helpful."

I paid the bill, and we started back.

"I'm pregnant," she said after several minutes of silence.

"You're going to be a mother?"

She looked at me with a slight grin. "It's amazing how fast you pick these things up."

The next morning the missionaries had a memorial

service for Ryan. Jill and I sat on the front row and listened to them talk and sing. After it was over, they came around and shook our hands and said how much they loved Ryan. Looking at them, I suddenly saw them differently than ever before in my life. They were clean and I was not. They had faith and I had none. Sitting there, feeling estranged from the Church, from my sister and my dead brother, I sadly realized—I've come a long way, baby.

We left Italy the same day. After we'd reached our cruising altitude, Jill pulled out a packet of papers and gave them to me.

"What's this?"

"Pedigree sheets. It shows our family line."

"I don't care about that. Save it for your kid."

"I have other copies."

A flight attendant asked if I'd like a drink. Because of Ryan and Jill, I said no.

I looked at the names in pyramid fashion on the pages. "Good grief, Jillsy, this is hard-core genealogy."

She went through the pages name by name, filling in lives as she went. I politely nodded my head until she showed me a picture of my grandmother on her wedding day. You think of grandparents as old, because that's what they are when you come along. But in the picture she was young and beautiful, eighteen years old with a blush in her cheeks (although the black and white picture couldn't bring it out), standing in front of a wedding cake.

"You look like her."

She looked at the picture. "I thought so too."

"She's beautiful. I'd marry a girl who looked like that."

"But she wouldn't marry you, at least not until you shape up."

"For a girl like her, I'd change."

She looked at me with raised eyebrows. "Yeah?"

"I'm serious. I know I have disgusting habits. It's just that right now I'm in my disgusting phase. But I'll change someday."

The flight attendant brought our lunch. I couldn't open the plastic food packets. They're designed so only a gorilla can open them.

"You think of our ancestors as being alive somewhere?" I asked her during dessert.

She nodded. "I think they welcomed Ryan back when he died."

"And they know about us?"

"Especially you."

"Why me?"

"You're the last male in the line who can raise up sons to carry on the family name. Jimmy, they want you to carry on the line."

I looked at her. She was serious.

"I'll think about it, okay?"

"Fair enough. And when I get more information about our ancestors, I'll send it."

I picked up my copy of the family records. "It is kind of interesting."

"Admit it, you're fascinated."

We arrived in Idaho the next day with the casket on the plane with us. Scott met us at the airport. He and Jill kissed enthusiastically; then he shook my hand. He was tanned and his hands were strong, and he wore a Cenex cap and Levi's and a western shirt. He was running his uncle's place while they were on a mission. We drove to their place in a nearly new pickup.

They lived in a farmhouse.

"I'm kind of sleepy," Jill said at nine o'clock.

"Me too," Scott said.

They went to bed. I stayed in the living room and watched TV, dozing off and then coming to during another program.

I wanted a drink in the worst way, but I'd promised

myself I wouldn't drink in their home. Besides, I knew
they wouldn't have any around.

About eleven I went to the bathroom to get ready for
bed. After going through the same ritual Zinia had
taught me, I opened the medicine cabinet. I enjoy looking in people's medicine cabinets. You can learn so
much. There was a woman's style razor for shaving legs.
Next to it was a bottle of English Leather, recreating the
smell I'd caught earlier in the night when Scott came out
of the bathroom heading for bed. There were some vita-
min pills for pregnancy, two toothbrushes—his would be
the tan one, hers light green.

It was late but I couldn't sleep. I wandered around
the living room. I found their wedding album on a shelf
and looked through it. There were several pictures of
them taken outside the Idaho Falls Temple, arm in
arm—embracing in front of the temple, a closeup of her
looking into his eyes.

I turned a page, and although it was Jill, the picture
looked very much like the picture of our grandmother
on the day of her wedding—the same high cheekbones,
the same long hair and shy smile I'd seen in the picture
Jill had shown me on the plane.

Jill and her grandmother were beauties. The pattern
had repeated itself from one generation to another.

What about the men in the family? Was I similar to
any of them?

Rummaging through the bookshelf, I found several
old photo albums. They were of Scott's family. There
were lots of pictures of men and women and children,
pictures taken many years ago. There was a saucy young
couple posing in front of a Model T Ford. I decided it
must be Scott's grandparents. Another picture showed
them at a miniature village, because the woman, still in
her twenties, had an impudent expression as she peeked
over the roof of a house.

There was a picture of a baby held by the woman, and after that, with each page, I could see the woman and the husband occasionally shown, grow older. Little by little the children grew. The one was joined by two others in the pictures. The boy would grow up to be Scott's father.

There was another album showing Scott's parents outside the Salt Lake Temple, and then a picture of Scott, chubby, cherubic Scott, growing up.

Some of the later pictures had me and Scott in them. There was a picture of Scott and Jill on the night of the junior-senior prom. More pictures of them and then a picture of Scott in a missionary blue suit outside the missionary training building in Provo. The last page on the album had a wedding announcement for Scott and Jill.

Families moving through time like an endless tide.

Finally I fell asleep watching TV on the couch. When I woke up at seven, I heard voices in the kitchen. Still lying on the couch, I saw Scott sitting at the kitchen table, and Jill, still in an old terry cloth robe, was frying some bacon and eggs. Her hair was still mussed from sleep, and she kept brushing it back out of her eyes. She scooped the food from the pan onto the plate and came around in back of her husband and set it down in front of him, pausing to tousle his hair and hug him. He reached out and held her hand and smiled at her. She kissed him, then asked if he wanted any orange juice.

Seeing Jill in her frayed robe, content with love for her husband, sleepily setting out a dish of bacon and eggs for him, her tummy just beginning to puff out with their future child—I wanted to have a life like theirs.

Life ought to be more than passing strangers in the hall and saying, "Hey, how's it going? How about those Dodgers, hey?"

It suddenly made sense for a man to promise to be faithful to just one woman, and for her to make the same promise to him, and for them to fuse together to produce children, and the children grow up in a stable home where they can be loved, until one day the children leave and start the process all over again.

Ryan's funeral was at ten o'clock. A church leader from Salt Lake City spoke at the funeral and assured us Ryan was all right and his test was over. He said that Ryan had been welcomed by his ancestors on the other side, and that he was happy where he was, and that someday he would be resurrected and live on the earth again.

The strange thing about it was, I believed him.

Later in the day Scott took me for a drive. We drove around looking at the high school and the drive-in. We drove by what had been Logan's place. Now it was a housing development. There was Fred Avenue and Ruth Drive and Rachel Circle.

We stopped at the drive-in for a hamburger and fries. Teenagers played video games inside.

"Make you feel old to be here again?" he asked.

"I guess so."

"Ever play those games?"

"Not much."

"Bet you a milkshake I can beat you."

I grinned. "You're on, cowboy."

Fifteen minutes later it was as if the years had rolled away and we were back together again, punching each other in the shoulder and bragging incessantly.

On the way back he asked, "How do you like my pickup?"

"It's okay to haul pigs around in, but if you want to talk vehicles, let's talk about a Porsche."

"Is that what you drive?"

"No, not yet. But soon."

"The day you drive a Porsche is the day chickens bark."

"It's on order!"

He laughed. "For when? Thirty years from now?"

"You'll see. Someday I'll drive it up here and show you a real car."

We both started laughing.

It felt good to have a friend again.

The next day Scott and Jill drove me to the airport. I had two drinks on the plane. A few hours later I was back in California.

CHAPTER SIX

I lived in a singles complex, complete with swimming pool and volleyball court and coed sauna. The day I arrived home from Idaho, there was a party going on down by the swimming pool. One of the guys was getting married the next day. There were plenty of free drinks. I drank and told jokes. Later I floated on an inner tube in the middle of the pool with a drink cradled carefully in my hand.

Ah, the good life, I thought contentedly.

There was a noise.

I woke up.

Two men in suits were peering down at me.

"Good morning," one of them said brightly.

I looked around. It was daytime. My feet were sprawled out across the sidewalk, and my head was under a rosebush.

"Beautiful day, isn't it?" the other one said.

I moved. My head felt as if someone had carved a jack-o-lantern in it. I moaned.

"We were just dropping by on folks in this neighborhood today, and we saw you there. Did you fall? Are you all right?"

"Trimming the roses," I muttered. "Can you get me up? I seem to have gotten stuck."

They helped me up. I looked at them. They were Mormon missionaries.

"Do you live here?" one of them asked.

I slowly looked around.

"We'd like to share an important message with you. Would it be better out of the sun?"

"Of course. We can go to my apartment."

I was trying to get my bearings. All the apartments looked the same.

"Forget where you live?" one of them asked politely.

"No, of course not. I know where I live."

It was all coming back to me now. I lived on the second floor in number 213. I gingerly moved up the stairs.

"You've got a bad bruise on your leg. How'd you get it?"

I stopped and looked down. The back of my leg was purple. I didn't remember how it'd happened.

"Baseball," I said.

We stood in front of the door. "My roommate's a slob," I said.

I didn't have a roommate, but I knew what shape the room was in.

"That's okay," one of them said.

I fumbled around in my swimsuit pocket looking for a key, then realized the door was unlocked. I opened the door. A dog lunged at me. I shut the door. The dog crashed against the door and barked viciously.

"Good watchdog, I bet," one of the elders said.

I didn't have a dog.

I smiled and nodded my head. "Very good."

A few minutes later, my next-door neighbor, a tall dancer with a slim figure and her hair done into a braided ponytail, came up the stairs with a bag of groceries. Her name was Alicia and she preferred that, but I always called her Ali. I was sitting on the cement walkway holding my head while the two missionaries talked about what a nice day it was. You can always tell out-of-staters that way.

Ali spoke a mile a minute. "Jimmy! I'm so sorry. Oh, I should've told you, but your door was open and you were

down by the pool the way you'd been all night, so I
thought it'd be okay. See, what happened, Marty, this
guy I've been dating, keeps telling me about all the dan-
gers around L.A. Well, last night he gave me a Doberman
pinscher, and, well, I had to go out this morning, and I
thought if my roommate came in from working the night
shift at the hospital and saw the dog, she'd be really
scared, so I thought, well, I saw you down by the pool,
and I figured you'd be there most of the morning, and
your door was open. Boy, I'm really sorry." She looked at
my leg. "That was some fall you took off the diving board
last night, wasn't it! I'm surprised you can even walk
today. Let me look at your leg."

"It's my head that hurts."

She kissed me on my forehead. "Poor Jimmy. Hey,
but you were so much fun last night at the party. Well,
don't worry about the dog. I'll get it out right away. His
name is Spot."

"Spot? A Doberman pinscher doesn't have spots."

"Marty calls him Spot because of what he does to the
carpet," she said.

"Spot," she whispered at the door. "Nice doggie.
Spot, look, I'm going to open the door now. You be a nice
doggie now. I got your food."

She opened the door slowly. Spot was lying down,
chewing on a shoe.

"Stupid dog," I muttered.

Spot bared his teeth at me.

"C'mon, Spot, nice doggie," she said sweetly. Spot followed her out.

She left. Strewn all over the floor were the contents of
two bags of garbage, courtesy of Spot. Empty beer cans
and cardboard pizza containers were scattered everywhere.

"I see what you mean about your roommate," one of
the missionaries said.

I asked them to come back later. They said they would.

A few minutes later I knocked on Ali's door again. Spot lunged at the door. "Just a minute," she called out.

"Your dog scattered garbage all over," I said after she finally got the door open.

"Your forehead is sweating. Don't you feel well?"

"I feel lousy."

"Who are the guys in the suits?"

"Ministers. Are you going to clean up the mess or not?"

"Sure. Just a minute. Have you had your garlic yet today?"

She took garlic pills every day. She'd read that garlic helps fight disease. She claimed that as long as she took garlic pills, she never got sick. She did look amazingly healthy. I'd humored her along, and she got me to take some too. After that it became a ritual. Whenever she saw me, she gave me some. When I belched, it was enough to intimidate any germ.

While she cleaned up the garbage, I sat on the couch.

"Ali, are you ever going to get married?" I asked.

"Oh sure, sometime, but not now. I want to be free, to grow at my own pace, to actualize my essence, to be in tune with the rhythm of the times." She looked in the mirror. "Does my stomach look flatter than yesterday?"

"I can't tell."

"Why do you ask about marriage?"

"I don't know. Don't you ever want to be a regular person? You know, a regular married person. Maybe have a garden and raise string beans, or have a baby, or send out a family picture for your Christmas card. And at night you'd sort recipe cards, or something like that. Don't you ever wish that?"

She looked at me strangely. "You're still drunk from last night, aren't you."

I continued. "No, listen to me. You'd have the same man around all the time, and wouldn't be juggling from one to the other. And your husband would have a job, maybe he'd be a member of Kiwanis, and he'd change the oil in your car, and fix leaky faucets, and maybe once a year he'd go hunting. On Saturdays, after he'd mowed the lawn, he'd go down to a small store at the end of your lane, kind of a general store, and he'd just sit around and talk with some of the other men. Maybe they'd talk about the crops, like if there's been a drought, and maybe this is the driest year since 1952, or something like that. And if you got sick, he'd take care of you. And you'd have a robe, kind of an old robe, and flannel pajamas, and you wouldn't spend your life looking in the mirror every fifteen minutes to check out your stomach, because you'd have more important things to do. You ever think about that?"

She sat down next to me and reached over and held my hand. "What's wrong, Tiger?"

"My brother died this week. He was only nineteen years old."

"I'm really sorry. How did he die?"

I told her about his being a missionary, like the two who'd just been there, and that I was a member of the Church too, but not a good one.

"I went to the funeral and saw people with families and mortgages. And they're solid. My sister looks at me with that worried look sisters get. I woke up this morning, hung over, yet still wanting a drink. I'm killing myself. Why am I doing that?"

There was a knock at the door. I had her answer it. It was the missionaries again. I shook my head to indicate I didn't want to see them. She invited them in.

"I'm Elder Farnsworth," one said, shaking her hand as if she'd just won an Oscar.

"And I'm Elder Blake," the less-experienced elder piped up.

"I'm Alicia Alan. I live next door."

They came in.

"Jimmy Pepper," I said weakly, without getting up.

They gave us part of a discussion. She gave the answers while I nursed my head. "If you knew God had called a prophet in our own time, would that make a difference in your life?" Elder Farnsworth asked.

Ali said it would.

They asked if it would make a difference in my life.

I was rummaging through a shirt pocket. "Rats! I'm out of cigarettes."

"Nicotine fit?" Ali teased.

I sat back down. "It's no big thing. I don't need 'em."

Elder Farnsworth was the more experienced of the two missionaries. "I testify that God has sent us today with this message."

"Can I be perfectly honest?" I said. "I don't want His message. I just want Him to leave me alone. And that goes for you two. Now please get out of here."

The elders stood up.

Ali turned to me. "This is what your brother was doing?"

I nodded.

"I'd think you'd want to hear what they have to say."

"I've heard it all," I grumbled.

"Well, I haven't. It's interesting. I want to listen."

"Suit yourself." I started for the kitchen.

Elder Farnsworth wouldn't let me get away gracefully. "We'd like to come back another time when you feel better."

"Elders, you're wasting your time. I'm already a member. So we'll see you around at church sometime, okay?"

"Let me get your name so we can have home teachers visit," Elder Farnsworth said.

I cringed. Soon there'd be a parade of church officials at my door.

Elder Farnsworth had his pen poised. "Let's see, it's Jimmy . . ."

"Pepper," Alicia said with a smile.

"Brother Pepper," the younger elder said, "how do you feel about the Church?"

"Don't call me Brother Pepper," I groaned. "Give it up. Listen, give my regards to the Tabernacle Choir, okay?"

I went to the kitchen and took some aspirin.

Ali continued to meet with the missionaries. They always had their discussions at my place.

In just a short time, she'd made a commitment to quit drinking and smoking, and then the elders gave a lesson about living the ten commandments, one commandment in particular. She committed to live the principle of chastity.

The next night about two in the morning, after I'd returned from doing a bit at the Comedy Store, I passed her door and could hear a guy yelling at her. He sounded very mad.

I let myself into my apartment.

A minute later he put his fist through her large window, stormed off to his car, and drove away.

I went to see her window. She was looking at it too.

"That was Marty. I told him about chastity. He wasn't happy. Sometimes he gets mad when he's disappointed. He says he'll give me a day to think things over."

"And then what?" I asked.

"He didn't say, and I was afraid to ask."

"Anything I can do to help?" I asked.

She kissed me on the cheek lightly. "Jimmy, I sort of think of you like a brother. Don't worry—if I can think of anything, I'll let you know."

* * * * * * * * * * * *

Apparently Ali thought of something, because the next night when I returned, her dog Spot was shut up in my apartment, and there was a note telling me she'd decided to go back to her parents in Kansas, away from Marty. She also said she'd decided to be baptized.

Her note ended with, "Would you please keep Spot for me until Marty comes to get him?"

When Marty came for Spot, he accused me of being responsible for Ali being unavailable to him. Just as he was about to crack my head open with an empty bottle, Spot lunged toward him. Marty jumped quickly away, swore angrily at us, and then left.

"Good dog," I said gratefully.

A while later Ali wrote me and said how much being a member of the Church meant to her.

One morning about eleven o'clock I was sitting at the edge of the bed staring at the floor, holding my aching head, trying to work up enough energy to walk to the window and yell at the garbage men to quit banging the cans around so much. There was a knock at the door.

I forgot about Spot and opened the door. It was Elders Blake and Farnsworth. He rushed toward them, sniffing and growling.

"He doesn't like strangers," I said, grabbing his collar. He snapped at me. I jumped away.

"Strangers?" Elder Blake smiled. "He nearly bit you."

"He has a short memory."

"May we come in?" Elder Farnsworth asked.

"Gee, I don't know. I'm really kind of busy right now."

"Alicia wrote and asked us to see you," Elder Farnsworth said. I let them in. They gave me a letter from her. She asked me to listen to the missionary lessons as a personal favor to her.

I looked up from the letter.

"Just leave me alone," I muttered.

"You are alone," Elder Blake said.

He'd hit it on the head. I was alone.

"Please listen to our message," he said.

My shoulders slumped. "Why bother with me?"

"God hasn't given up on you yet," Elder Blake said, "so why should we?"

I let them give me a lesson.

"Okay, now what?" I asked when it was over.

"You pray and ask God if it's true."

"Anything else?"

"More than that—you need to really pour out your soul in prayer."

I smiled weakly. "There's nothing to pour. Maybe a few dribbles is all there's left."

Elder Blake laughed. Elder Farnsworth did not.

I loved Elder Blake from the first. He had a pimple on his nose. And he'd broken his shoelace and tied it together and was wearing it that way.

"We'd like you to offer the prayer," Elder Blake said.

How could I turn down Elder Blake? We knelt down.

I intended a nice little prayer, tidy and short. After all, I'd been to church as a boy and given little prayers. "Bless us to get something from the lesson, something to use in our everyday lives." That's what I intended for this prayer—but when I started, something happened. Deep inside of me, there was a feeling, something I'd forgotten, that mended and soothed and gave hope that I could return to the Church, to God, and to my family.

Somewhat embarrassed, I wiped my eyes and said amen.

Elder Blake hugged me, and Elder Farnsworth said they would help. They shook my hand vigorously, gave me some pamphlets to read, and then left.

The next day doubt cropped up. A battle raged inside me.

It couldn't be true. It's too wild.

But what if it is?

It isn't.

But what if it is?

It can't be true.

But what if it is?

It's not. If it were, more people would know about it.

But what if it is?

It isn't.

How do you know?

I just know.

How?

What about Fred kicking me out of the house in the middle of the night? He was a member of the Church, wasn't he?

Okay, but what about Rachel and Jeff? You could have stayed with them if you hadn't gotten so mad at Fred that night. You ran away even before letting Zinia know what was wrong. She never would've let you go that night if she'd known. And Logan and Zinia were good people. They believed the Church was true. Jill believes it's true. And Ryan died while teaching the gospel. What about them?

But it can't be true.

But what if it is? What if Christ speaks to mankind again? What if it's true?

I paused. If it's true, then it's important.

You can find out if it's true.

No, I can't. Not for sure.

The elders said you can.

What do they know? Nineteen-year-old kids. Would God trust a message like this to a nineteen-year-old kid?

And then it hit me.

Ryan had been a nineteen-year-old kid.

They gave me other lessons.

They prayed with me and testified to me. Eventually they gave me the lesson that teaches that alcohol and tobacco and coffee and tea are not good for us.

While they talked, I had the feeling that Ryan was in the room. Finally they paused. Elder Farnsworth looked at me steadily. "Will you live this commandment?" he asked. Elder Blake looked hopeful.

Painfully I said it for the first time—the thing that everyone around me was already saying. "I can't stop. I've tried, but it's out of control, and there's nothing I can do to stop."

They brought the bishop of the ward I lived in. He talked with me for a long time.

A day later two others came. They said they were my home teachers. They said they could help me get off booze. I said I didn't believe that. They said they'd once been heavy drinkers too, but they'd changed, and so could I.

They came every day about noon, just as I was getting up. Sometimes at night they'd stop by the Comedy Store and sit with me, three grown men nursing glasses of V-8 Juice.

I started going to church. The first time I entered the building, I felt as if I should have a sign warning that, although I had a tie on and had shaved off my beard, I was unclean.

I met once every Sunday for a few minutes with the bishop. We worked on repentance.

A Sunday sacrament meeting six months later. Two high-school-age boys have broken the bread into bite-size chunks while we've been singing a hymn. One of them kneels and offers a prayer over the bread. Twelve- and thirteen-year-old boys receive the trays of bread. They move quietly to their stations, and the trays are passed from one person to the other down the rows.

A tray comes to me. I pick up a small piece of bread and put it in my mouth.

I am alone with my thoughts. They say we should think about Jesus during this time, about His sacrifice for us. Somehow He took upon Him our sins. It's painful for me to think about that. I added much to His burden.

I'm sorry for my past. The strange thing is, when I was away from the Church, it didn't seem like what I did was so bad. I was basically a nice guy, wasn't I? But as I started back, the realization of how wrong I'd been came on strong.

There's a price we must pay to qualify for forgiveness. The price is a broken heart and a contrite spirit. For the alcoholic the contrite spirit means an admission that he is incapable of doing it alone, that he is helpless alone, that he must rely on higher power.

I made some bad mistakes, and I could make them again if I'm not careful.

The young boys carry the trays back to the table. The second youth kneels down and offers a prayer on the water.

Thanks, God, for making it possible for me to come back.

CHAPTER SEVEN

Months later, at my bishop's suggestion, I attended a three-day regional young adult conference at a college down the coast. Not knowing a soul there, still feeling unsure of myself at church, I registered and got a name-tag and room assignment. I requested and got a single room. I left Spot in my drab brown station wagon. I planned to sneak him into my room after dark.

Sitting at the tiny desk in the dorm room, I looked at the schedule of events. I had already missed the watermelon bust and swimming activity. Right then they were having a pie-eating contest, and after supper, there would be a dance.

Reading the schedule of events depressed me. It was all so lovely and homey—and boring. I slept through supper and part of the dance, then woke up at eight o'clock, thought about taking a shower for the dance, but decided it was too much trouble.

I hung on the fringes of the dance and watched. They were playing the bunny hop. Five hundred feet jumping in unison sounded like the building was about to come down.

A few minutes later I went to the car to give Spot some water and dog food. Then I decided to take him for a walk. Just as I'd put the leash on and was letting him out, I saw a woman in the parking lot doing the same thing with her dog. She was tall and outdoorsy-looking.

Our dogs barked energetically at each other. Spot

pulled at the leash, anxious to maim her small cocker
spaniel.

We smiled at each other.

"Walking your dog?" I asked.

"Sorry, I don't have a watch!" she shouted. She was
either deaf or didn't hear my question over the noise our
dogs were making.

I decided to try again. "We're in a fraternity!" I
yelled.

"What?" she shouted.

"Fraternity!" I yelled. "We're in a fraternity!"

"Who is?"

"We are! You and me!"

"Not me!" she shouted above the barking of the two
dogs. "Fraternities are too wild!"

"A fraternity of dog owners!" I shouted.

"What?"

Spot was really getting to me. "AH, SHUT UP!" He
quieted down. I said calmly to her, "We share common
interests."

She looked puzzled. "We do? What are they?"

The dogs started barking again.

"Dogs!" I shouted.

"Oh!" she said. We both laughed. It felt delicious to
laugh with her.

Our dogs traded mutual sniffs warily. She and I
smiled weakly, trying to ignore them as they went
through this strange ritual. In due time, they seemed
willing to accept each other.

"We could walk together," I said.

"Fine," she said.

We walked. She looked at the well-kept lawns while I
looked at her.

Her name was Amy Malone. I said it over and over in
my mind—it fit perfectly—wholesome, all-American
Amy Malone.

She was as tall as me, with short cropped blonde hair parted near the crown of her head. The part served as sort of the Continental Divide for hair—strands leaned either to the left or to the right with no deviating curls along the way.

Her thick eyebrows served as a beacon of her moods. Her face didn't appear to have much makeup; she had a scrubbed-clean appearance.

She talked. "They say you can tell a person by the kind of dog he has. A man with a collie would be gentle and wise. And let's see—a man with a Doberman pinscher—" She paused. "I bet you have searchlights on the roof of your house, don't you?"

My mouth dropped open. She has a sense of humor—she's my kind of woman. If a woman can have sensuous teeth, she had 'em. When she laughed, there they were, large, pearly, and white. Her motions were slow and fluid, and although she was walking as fast as I was, she gave the impression that her body was only at half speed, like a well-tuned Porsche slowing at a stop-light.

We left the campus and entered a residential area with large, ample homes and manicured lawns.

Spot started rummaging through somebody's garbage. He ripped open a plastic bag of garbage and began scattering things in the yard. I pulled on his leash, and he turned to snarl at me.

"C'mon, Spot," I pleaded. "Good dog. Spot, be reasonable." He continued scattering garbage. "You numbskull, you stupid dog," I muttered.

The owner of the lawn and the garbage opened his front door and yelled at me to get my dog out of there.

"What do you think I'm trying to do, you yo-yo!"

"I'm calling the cops! They'll lock you and your wolf up." He slammed his door.

I felt like an idiot having a dog I couldn't control. "You go ahead," I said to Amy, not wanting her to be arrested too. "I'll catch up later."

She shook her head. "You've got to show him who's boss."

"I don't blame him—a man hates to have garbage on his lawn."

She grinned. "I meant the dog. May I?" she asked, offering to take the leash from me.

"Don't!" I warned.

"Why not?"

"That dog is an animal."

She laughed. "I understand that."

"I'm serious."

She took the leash and said quietly but with authority, "Heel." Spot sat down beside her.

While she petted Spot, I restored the man's garbage back to some semblance of order. By the time the police arrived, everything was picked up. They let us go.

"What do you do?" she asked.

"I'm a comedian."

"Yeah, but what do you do for a living?"

"I'm a comedian."

She laughed. "Is your dog part of the act?"

"Hardly. What about you?"

"I'm a high school P.E. teacher. I coach girls' basketball."

"How does that work? A male coach tells his boys to go out there and kill the other team. What do you tell your girls?"

"To get more points."

I nodded. "Makes sense."

We continued our walk. She told me she was a convert to the Church of just three months. Nobody else in her family was a member.

After we had returned our dogs to the cars, we both grew silent, uncertain of where our acquaintance was heading.

"Can I walk you to the dance?"

"Okay," she said. We went inside, got some punch and cookies, and sat down to watch the others.

Later we danced. During a slow dance, I put my arms around her and shifted from one foot to the other in time with the music. She melted into my arms. It was very nice.

When the song was over, she asked if I were Italian. I said no. She said she smelled garlic.

I popped a Certs into my mouth. "I take garlic pills."

"What for?"

"They keep me healthy. I'm never sick."

"Sure, sure," she laughed.

We sat down.

"I have a confession to make," I said. "I'm not really a comedian. I'm actually in town on business. I'm starting a new airlines—Generic Airlines. Our planes'll be in plain brown wrappers."

All the women I'd ever known before would have just smiled tolerantly. But not her. She climbed into my fantasy with me. "I've heard of it," she said. "Your motto isn't 'Fly the Friendly Skies.' Your motto is 'So what did you expect at these prices?'"

She says funny things. I loved her already.

"Right," I continued. "Inside the plane, we have no seats, just straps to hold onto, like in a subway. Before the plane takes off, our flight attendant comes on and says, 'There are emergency exits on the plane, but we're not telling where they are. If anything goes wrong, the crew want to be the first ones out.'"

"Yeah," she smiled, "and during the flight, you don't serve a meal. What you do is roll a peanut butter jar down the aisle, and anyone who stops it can eat."

Being with her was like when you go to scout camp and you get on the buddy system, and it turns out your assigned buddy, who you thought would be a nerd, turns out to like to horse around and tell jokes and be a general goof-off—just like you. So even when it's raining and you have to stay in a tent that leaks, you're still trading off stories and jokes to each other as fast as you can.

It's interesting about the big and little decisions in life. It took me four months to decide whether I wanted waxed or unwaxed dental floss, but in half an hour I was positive I'd found the woman I wanted to marry.

We got going on some ad-lib role playing. The first one was a bishop phoning Lot just after his wife was turned into a pillar of salt. I was the bishop and Amy was Lot.

"Hello, Brother Lot, is your wife there?" I said.

"Ah, no, bishop," she said. "Well, that is, she's here, but she's not taking phone calls now."

"Well, I just wanted to thank her for helping with the church supper. You know, your wife is really a pillar in our community."

"Bishop, that's so true."

"She's a rock, your wife."

Amy faked extreme sadness. "I know, I know. Isn't it terrible? She looked back and was turned into a pillar of salt."

"Where is she?" I asked.

"Well, she's just outside here. I can see her from the window. HEY, GET AWAY FROM THERE! . . . Excuse me, bishop, the cows were licking her arm. It's okay now."

"This must've really been a shock to you, Lot."

"Everything happened all at once. First we lose our home to the fire, then we have to leave Sodom. And now this . . ."

"Well, that's the way things go sometimes. When it rains, it pours."

We never finished. We were both laughing too hard.

God had sent me a woman. Or sent her a man. Or

sent us to the dance. Or got our dogs together. One way
or the other I'd found her, and I was never going to let
her go. Think about it, a woman who laughed at my
jokes.

How can I describe the way she made me feel? It was
the way you feel when you're a kid and you go over to
your best friend's house. His mother opens the door, and
you say, "Can Davey come out to play?" And she says yes.
And the moment you see him, you know you're going to
have a great day playing guns or space people, and that
in a while his mom, who's a chubby woman who smiles
even at kids, is going to give you both some fresh-baked
chocolate chip cookies and milk. And later in the afternoon when it's hot out, you and Davey are going to climb
a big oak tree in the backyard and pretend to be a family
of chipmunks and be hidden in the summer leaves.
Davey is your best friend in the whole world.

That's what it was like to be around her.

But that's not all.

It was the feeling that we'd become good friends, and
then fall in love, and then get married. It was the feeling
that changing my rotten habits had been necessary before I could meet her, that God forgave me for all the rotten things I'd done, and to show He loved me, He let me
find a woman like Amy.

In the meantime it was being aware of all the little delicious messages being sent out, watching her smile, feeling the warmth of her hand as I pretended to read her
fortune, enjoying the little pleasures of being around a
terrific-looking woman. Maybe because I knew there
would be only little pleasures for a while, it made me
more sensitive to her. It was knowing that all the delicious senses activated by a man and woman being close to
each other were put there to be enjoyed as long as we
stayed within the proper limits.

"Let's be silly," I said, pulling her into the cultural
hall.

We went to the microphone. It was between dances. "Testing, testing. May I have your attention, please? I'm a dance coach for Universal Studios, and they've asked me to teach you some of the dances featured in upcoming movies. Can we get everyone out on the floor now?"

We waited for couples to come out.

"The first dance we want to teach you is called Sore Toe. It'll be coming out in January with the release of a sequel to *Saturday Night Fever,* called *Monday Morning Headache.* Now what you do is pretend you've just stepped on a nail. You hobble forward two steps, then hobble back two steps, then reach down and touch your foot. My assistant and I will demonstrate it for you. Could we have some music now?"

Someone put on a record, and Amy and I did the Sore Toe.

"Now everybody try it."

Picture several hundred people gimping around to music, and you'll appreciate why Amy had to excuse herself to go laugh in the hall.

A young woman came up to me. "I've got a question. What foot should you pretend is sore?"

"The left," I said with authority. "Always the left in America. In Europe, of course, they do it with the right. But that's called Continental Sore Toe."

"Thank you," she said sincerely.

A few minutes later Amy and I went out on the dance floor and just rocked back and forth and held each other.

The dance was over at twelve-thirty. We had half an hour before we had to be in our dorms. My plan was to see if I could at least kiss her goodnight. But first we had to help each other sneak our dogs into our dorm rooms. Her room was on the first floor of Palmer Hall. She went inside and opened her window, and I handed her dog, Clyde, to her. Then we went to my dorm, and she talked to the guy at the desk while I let Spot chase me up the back stairs.

By the time we finally arrived at her dorm again, it was five minutes to one, and a chaperon was standing at the door, officially clearing her throat.

Amy melted into my arms. Then she sniffed and pulled away. "You smell like a dog," she said.

I scowled. "That's gotta be the least romantic sentence in the world."

We both started laughing. It ruined the mood for the other couples.

"It's exactly 12:58," our chaperon called out, getting ready to lock the doors.

"I was going to try to kiss you," I said as she edged closer to the door as I advanced.

"And I was going to let you," she said.

"Look, if I can find a clothespin within the next two minutes, will you kiss me?"

She laughed and shook her head.

"How about if we hold our noses?"

"I can't kiss and hold my nose at the same time."

"When can I see you again?"

"There's the fireside tomorrow morning," she said.

"Before that."

"I'm going jogging at six in the morning."

"Terrific. I'll meet you here at six. I'll wear a different pair of slacks and take a shower."

"Do you jog?" she asked.

"Every day."

"When did you start?" she asked suspiciously.

"Tomorrow."

The chaperon announced "One o'clock." Amy hurried inside.

"Wait a minute!" I called to her.

"Yes?"

"Suppose Johnny Carson joined the Church and later was called to be a church leader in Salt Lake City. He's giving his first major address in the Tabernacle. Go ahead."

"The world is full of wickedness," she began.

"How wicked is it?" I called out.

She started laughing. "It's so wicked . . . that . . ."

The chaperon closed and locked the door.

The next morning I knew I was in trouble when I saw her with a stopwatch. "What's that for?"

"To time myself. I usually go five miles."

"In a day?"

"I'll go slower today, so we can talk."

She wore lavender sweat pants, a pink sweat shirt with crew neck, and an expensive pair of running shoes. I wore a pair of Hush Puppies, black socks, a pair of jeans whose legs I'd cut off to the knees just a few minutes before, and a torn grease-stained sweat shirt I found in my car during the night.

It was a nice morning, the earliest I'd gotten up since I'd left Idaho. Because I was so slow, she ran circular patterns around me so she wouldn't get too far ahead of me. Soon the only sounds were me gasping wildly for air. She stopped.

"We can walk for a while," she said.

"Sure, go ahead," I gasped, "if you need to."

It took me five minutes to breathe normally again.

"I hope you don't think I'm intimidated by your athletic ability," I said, using my macho voice. "There are some sports that men just naturally do better in than women."

There were fireworks in her eyes. "Yeah? Like what?"

"You ever notice that all the world-class spitters are men? If you want, we can chalk out a line and see who can spit the farthest."

She laughed. "I concede."

While we walked she told me more about herself. She was raised in California and had gone to San Jose State College, where she majored in P.E. She learned about the Church when friends invited her to a church social.

"Being from L.A., you can guess what I thought when they asked me to a potluck. But they seemed like nice people, so I decided to risk it. It was the best thing I ever did."

By Sunday afternoon the conference was over. I helped carry Amy's suitcase to her car, although she was in better shape to do it than I was. Her dog, Clyde, was sitting in the front seat. Spot was in my car, which I'd pulled next to hers.

I put her suitcase in the trunk and closed it.

"So," I said, "the end of a perfect weekend."

"Really," she said with a reserved smile.

"I enjoyed getting to know you," I said.

"Me too," she said. "They say they're having another one of these in three months. Maybe we'll see each other then."

That was depressing. I'd die if I didn't see her before then.

Spot started barking as someone approached the car next to mine.

"Ah, pipe down!" It did no good—it never did. But it made me feel better to yell at him.

She started to get in her car.

"Please don't go," I said, letting my feelings show.

She nodded. "I feel the same way, but I have to leave sometime. I have to work tomorrow."

"Can I see you this weekend?" I asked.

"Friday night?"

"Sure."

"I'll give you my address." She fumbled in her purse for a piece of paper and a pen.

I looked at her. She had a nice nose, and her neck was exceptionally graceful looking. She looked wholesome and streamlined and clean-cut. And she smelled of Dial soap. She was just terrific.

"Does your team do a lot of fast breaks?" I asked.

"Yes, why?"

I smiled. "I just knew you'd be a fast-break kind of coach."

"Come to one of our games when the season starts."

"I will."

"I guess I'd better go." She got into her car.

"Wait!" I said.

"Yes?"

"I didn't get to kiss you last night. Do I get a rain check?"

She looked around. Suddenly the parking lot seemed to be full of church leaders.

She pursed her lips.

"I don't usually do this," she said, getting out of her car.

"I understand."

She stood close to me, her hands at her side, looking vulnerable. "One thing you should know—I don't play games."

I smiled. "Can I trust a coach who says she doesn't play games?"

"You know what I mean," she said.

"Maybe. You don't kiss a guy unless . . ."

She completed the sentence. "Unless I think I'm falling in love with him."

I reached out to hold her hand. "Okay—you don't play games, and I don't kid around."

"A comedian who doesn't kid around," she said quietly.

I kissed her.

When we broke apart, I was dizzy. It was like overdosing on Dial soap.

We kissed again. It was nice kissing someone my own height.

"I'd really better go now," she said, fumbling with the door. She was as spaced out as I was—possibly from the garlic.

Suddenly I realized she was going to leave me. I wouldn't see her for a whole week. It was like being five years old on a beautiful summer morning and you go to your very best friend's house with ideas about playing all day, and you knock on the door and nobody's home, and the next-door neighbor tells you they've gone on vacation for two weeks, and then you realize your best friend is gone, and two weeks seems like an eternity. That was how far away Friday seemed to me.

"So, until Friday," I said glumly.

"Friday," she said, getting in the car. "I want to thank you for a wonderful weekend."

She started to drive away. I watched the car pull out.

Crazily I ran after her down the street. "Amy! Stop!" I shouted.

She pulled over. "What's wrong?"

Out of breath, I gasped, "Can I possibly see you sooner than Friday?"

"How much sooner?" she asked.

"Much sooner."

She parked. I reached out and touched her arm. Clyde started to growl at me. She ordered him to be quiet.

"What do you suggest?" she asked.

I paused briefly to consider how foolish I was becoming, then plunged full speed ahead. "Do your parents happen to have a spare guest bedroom, or a couch that makes up into a bed, or even a sleeping bag, or three extra blankets, or a hammock in the backyard, or an abandoned car with a back seat, or a tree with a large branch . . ."

She was laughing again. "When can you come?"

"Right away," I said. "I'll follow you home. But look, I'll just stay a couple of days and I won't eat much."

"But what about your work?" she asked.

"I'll make arrangements."

* * * * * * * * * * * *

When we pulled up to her house, she suggested she go in first and tell her parents they were having a house guest. In a few minutes she came out and escorted me in.

It was an old house in what had once been a nice area but was now slowly degenerating. On the front porch by the door was a note pad that read, "If at home you do not find us, leave a note that will remind us." I cringed. She came from one of those knickknack families.

Her father was a fixer of things, a worker, a man you call when your washer goes out, a man you spend twenty minutes with discussing the weather, a man who takes pride in locks locked, a hard day's honest work for a day's pay. A man who listens to Lawrence Welk and then tells people he likes classical music. A factory worker who attends union meetings and reads the monthly newsletter. And his name was Ed.

Ed's wife was a woman who wears an apron, a woman who grows African violets in the windowsills of her home, who saves string, who sends off her entry blank to the *Reader's Digest* sweepstakes every time and after all these years still believes she's going to win, a woman whose greatest hope for her yet unmarried daughter is that she marry somebody who gets a weekly check with time-and-a-half for overtime. She actually attended PTA meetings while her children were in school, a woman who doesn't go to church but who listens faithfully every Sunday on the radio to the sermons and sends in a little money now and then to help them out. And her name was Dotty.

By the time we arrived, it was late. We put Spot and Clyde in the fenced backyard, where they'd be free to run around and ruin the lawn.

Her parents had eaten supper, so we made do with the leftovers. The kitchen was small and tidy with hand-painted yellow cupboards and an old, too-small refrigerator that just had a new compressor put in, because Ed couldn't throw anything away if it still worked. We ate while her parents watched TV, and every once in a while, her mother came in and asked if I'd like some pickles.

On Monday morning I got up to run with Amy before she left for work. I was going to stay another day, but just after she left in the morning, I called my agent.

"Where have you been?" he complained. "I've been trying all weekend to get in touch with you. I've got you a job in Vegas in a lounge. It's for three weeks, and it starts in two days. You're going to have to leave today."

"That's nice," I said calmly.

"What do you mean, nice? This is what we've been waiting for! What better thing you got to do anyway?"

"I'm in love, Bernie."

"Love, shmove. You get to Vegas today, you hear me? That's what's important."

Tuesday I opened. It wasn't one of the headliner acts in the city. Actually it was a lounge, a small bar in a hotel, sort of a poor man's Las Vegas. People liked my act, and by the end of the week I was starting to pull in people due to word of mouth.

I phoned Amy every night and we talked. The Bell system loved our phone calls. When I paid my bill, it allowed them to send up another communications satellite.

Sometimes on the phone we did crazy skits, like we were spies trading coded information.

"The Armenian cow treads amber waves of grain into iron sprockets," I whispered slowly to her.

"Ah," she said knowingly. "The burgomaster carries a bowl of soup on a leash."

"You're too much," I howled.

"You too," she said.

Friday afternoon she called me. I was taking a nap in my room.

A voice whispered, "The burgomaster has arrived."

"You're here?"

"In the lobby with a friend from my ward."
"I'll be right down!"

We had supper, the three of us. Her friend, Sharon, was nice, but a little slow to pick up on Amy and me.

I got them good seats for my monologue. It was as good as I'd ever done, but there was a problem. Some of the material in the monologue was risqué. The audience laughed, but Amy looked uncomfortable. After I finished, I sat down with her. She looked like she was going to cry. I asked if anything was wrong, and she said she had a headache.

After hearing my jokes, Sharon treated me as if I had the plague. She left as soon as she could. Amy and I went outside for a walk.

"Want anything to eat?" I asked.

"No, thanks," she said quietly.

"How about an ice cream cone?"

"No, thanks."

"Mind if I get one?"

"Go ahead."

I bought one and took a bite. She watched me carefully.

"Why are you looking at me like that?"

"To see if you eat with the same mouth you use to tell those jokes."

I quit eating. "It's what they want to hear. It doesn't mean anything. I don't even think about it anymore."

"How can you do this six days a week and then go to church on Sunday? Doesn't your conscience ever bother you?"

I cleared my throat nervously. "It's not permanent. After I get established, I'll change my act so it'll be good enough for church. I promise."

"You know it's wrong though, don't you? I mean, deep inside, you know."

We walked one whole block without talking.

"It's what comedians do in Vegas—they tell that kind of joke."

"Jimmy, there's plenty of decent people in the world who like clean jokes," she said.

"But, Amy, listen to me, they don't go to nightclubs. They go to PTA meetings."

"Somehow I expected more of you than just being like everybody else."

"C'mon, give me a break. It's just like an actor reading his lines. You think they arrest Macbeth for murder every night?"

"It's not the same. It's your monologue. You decide what to say."

I shook my head. "That's not really true. The audience decides. I've got to play to what they want. Please try to understand."

I started to put my arm around her but she pulled away. "Why do you want to hold me? Need more material for the show?"

I wiped my forehead. "Boy, you're really making me feel stress. You want to know something—stress causes sickness. What if I get sick? You think people'll pay to see a man blow his nose? This is my big chance. I can't get sick, and I can't change my act." I reached into my pocket and pulled out a couple of garlic pills and swallowed them. "Want one? You must be feeling stress too, right now."

"There's a difference—my conscience doesn't bother me."

"Let's just walk for a while and not talk, okay?"

"All right."

At least she let me hold her hand. We walked down the Las Vegas Strip, glowing with promises of pleasure. Outside the hotel where I worked was a sign with my name on it. My name in Las Vegas—it was what I'd dreamed about since junior high school.

"I don't have an education or any skills. There's nothing else I can do. If I don't make it here, I don't make it."

Finally she started crying. "I expected more from you."

"You and my sister'd really get along."

We were at the door to her room. This was the girl I wanted to marry, and she was embarrassed because of the one thing in my life I did well. We didn't even kiss goodnight.

I need a drink, I thought, as I left her hotel on foot. Just one to calm my nerves. I deserve it. Just this one time'll be okay. Just to help me get through this.

I can't have a drink, I answered. Never again in my life. No matter what happens. I can never have a drink.

Just one.

I'll take a walk instead.

I spent the night walking, trying to fight the urge to have a drink. By the time the sun came up, I was ten miles outside of town.

Walking back, I found a cafe and had breakfast and phoned my sister and told her about Amy.

"So that's it," I said. "Tell me what to do."

"How bad are the jokes?"

I told her one.

She moaned. "Good grief, Jimmy."

"This is Vegas. That goes over very big here."

"What's worth more to you, Amy or that crummy joke?"

I spent a week trying to work up an act that was clean. I tried it out on a Tuesday night.

After it was over, the manager, a guy named Maury, came up to me. "What's wrong with the old stuff?"

"I decided to leave out the sex jokes."

"Are you crazy? This isn't Sesame Street."

"What about Bill Cosby? His material's clean, and he packs 'em in all the time."

"Cosby made it first with his comedy records. Now he's like a national shrine. People come a thousand miles just to hear him do the old stuff like 'Noah,' or 'Fat Albert.' So he gets away with it. But you can't. Do what everybody else does."

"Maury, work with me. I'll develop enough clean material to do an album. When it sells, you'll have exclusive rights to me in Vegas."

He shook his head. "Let's get something straight here. If you don't use the material you've been using, then you're finished. And not only here. I'll get you blackballed from every club in town. You'll never work again."

We had reached the bottom line. "I'm not going to use the old stuff anymore," I said.

"Then get outa here, hotshot," he grumbled. "Don't even stay for the second show. I'll run stag movies. That's about right for this crowd. Oh yeah, take a good look at Vegas on your way out. It's the last time you'll ever work here."

Half an hour later I left.

Las Vegas looks so beautiful at night.

CHAPTER EIGHT

We checkerboarded county roads for sixty madcap miles before losing the photographer from the 'National Inquirer.' When we arrived in Cody, we rented a pickup truck as a disguise.

"I can't call him Dad," I agonized as we left Worland, one hundred miles from Buffalo.

"What're you going to call him?"

"Hank."

She studied me. "Basically, what's your problem?"

"I hate him, Jill."

After being fired from Las Vegas, I returned to Los Angeles and got a small part in a movie about a giant fly that terrorizes the world. My part was to scream in three languages.

I continued to date Amy.

One night we were kissing in my car outside her house. She liked to kiss as much as I did, but she had better self-control about when it was time to go in.

"I'd better go in now."

"Already?" I complained. "I hate saying goodnight. Whataya say we get married. It'd be good for the dogs. They get lonely during the day. If we were married, they could sit around and chew our shoes while we were gone."

She looked at me quizzically. "Are you serious?"

"About marriage? I've known it from the first day I met you. I love you, wow, a lot. I've just been waiting for you to catch up. Miss Amy Malone, I respectfully request your hand in marriage."

She said she'd prayed about me, having heard of others who'd received special confirmations of whom they'd marry. "But nothing happened," she said, "except I noticed I couldn't stand the thought of *not* being married to you. Finally I decided that was my answer. I'd love to be your wife."

"Yahoo!" I shouted, in a manner befitting a Wyoming native.

We both started giggling like kids. It was a good old time until we saw her mother turn on the porch light and stare out at us.

We sobered up.

"There's a couple of things we need to iron out first," she said.

I smiled. "I'll iron anything."

"Where will we get married?" she asked.

"How long till you're a member a year and can go to the temple?" I asked.

"Six months."

The thought of clenching my teeth for six months was depressing. "Maybe we should think about a civil ceremony first."

Her enthusiasm dampened. "Of course, some people'll be disappointed we aren't getting married in the temple."

"Oh, who?" I asked.

"Me," she said quietly.

"I'd like to get married soon," I complained.

"I understand," she said.

"You do?"

"I teach health, you know."

"Sorry to be a prisoner of my glands," I said.

"I have glands too."

My eyebrows raised. "Yeah?"

She nodded. "We're getting to the place where it'd be more convenient to be married."

"Amy, I've had my quota of mistakes. I can't make any more. If you and I ever did anything wrong—well, we just can't, that's all."

"I know."

I sat and thought. "Maybe, though, if we both worked at it so we didn't get into trouble, maybe I could wait. You know, cold showers and all. It'd be character building, I guess. You ever notice—things that build character are never any fun."

"What would we have to do differently?" she asked.

I paused. "Well, suppose we went to a movie. I'd knock on the door and you'd come out, and you'd drive in your car and I'd drive in my car, and we'd go to the movie, and then if we went to eat, we'd both drive there, and when we came back to your place, we'd walk up to your front door and kiss goodnight using a timer."

Her eyes opened wide. "You're kidding."

"Nope."

We held each other and thought about it.

"Well," she said, "I guess the real question is what does God want us to do?"

We fasted and talked to our bishops and decided God wanted us to take a lot of cold showers and waste gasoline by driving two cars to the movies and using a three-minute timer, and never be alone in a room together, and not see anything but Muppet movies, and for me not to put suntan lotion on her back and legs at the beach even when she asked me to, and a bunch of other dumb things that kept us physically apart.

We decided to prepare for a temple marriage.

Out of respect for her father, she requested that I ask his permission to marry his daughter. I told her nobody does that anymore. She said we do.

So one day, feeling like a fool, I went to the garage to

talk to her father. He was underneath his car draining oil into a bucket.

"I'd like to talk to you, if I might, sir."

He rolled out from underneath the car and looked at me. "What's up?"

"Well, as you know, I've been, that is, Amy and me . . ."

"Excuse me." He rolled back under the car. "Be with you in a minute."

"Take your time, sir."

I stood and waited. A few minutes later he rolled back out and stood up, then proceeded to pour in some new oil. "Go ahead with whatever you were saying."

"Amy and I have been, well, shall we say, close."

He stared quizzically at me. "How close?"

"Not that close. That is, I, well, we'd like to, that is, in a manner of speaking, we, I mean, I . . . would like to ask your permission to marry your daughter . . . Amy, that is. She said I should ask."

We both sighed. "I see. Well . . ."

"So it's okay with you?" I said quickly, hoping for a quick exit.

"I'd like to know more about you. What are your career plans?"

"I'm going to put out a comedy record. Bill Cosby really wasn't a star until after his first record. If you hit it just right, you can make a lot of money with a record."

He opened another can of oil and poured it in, making sure not to waste a drop. "And what if you don't hit it just right?"

I paused. "I'm going to make it big. I just know it. See, making people laugh is important to me. I mean, it's all I've ever wanted to do."

"You're talking marriage. You'll probably have kids. How will you provide for 'em? Have you ever thought about going to college like Amy did?"

"I just want to be a comedian. It's what I do—my profession, I guess you'd say."

"So Amy ends up supporting your family while you putter around telling jokes to American Legion conventions?"

"That won't happen. I promise. If I have to, I'll get a job."

"What do you mean, if you have to."

I paused. "Okay, I'll get a job before we get married and work on my album the other sixteen hours a day."

"Can I be perfectly honest?"

I cringed. "Only if you have to."

He paused briefly. "Don't misunderstand me—I like you. You're good company, fun to be around. And it's clear you've charmed Amy. I've seen her light up when you walk in the room—"

I cut him off. "Thanks for being so honest. Can I go now?"

"I'm not through. You have no education and no trade to fall back on. What happens to comedians who don't make it?"

I sighed. "I can't think about that. I've got to succeed."

"Amy says you lost your job in Vegas because you refused to use dirty jokes anymore. What's that done to your career?"

"I'm on their blacklist. But if my record album does well—"

"Do you ever wish you were still working in Las Vegas?"

I shook my head. "If I were still at Vegas, then I wouldn't have Amy. I really do love her."

He looked strangely at me. "When I first met you, I wondered if there was anything beneath that smooth veneer. But there is, isn't there. It looks to me like you've got character."

"If I can marry your daughter, I'm sure I'll become a real character. That is, I'll develop real character."

He laughed. "I see why Amy's flipped for you. Go ahead. Marry my daughter."

I ran in to see her. "Let's get married!" I yelled.
"Yahoo!" she shouted.

Amy's father got me a job as a night watchman at the
place where he used to work. My job was to watch and
make sure only mice scurried through a warehouse. I'd
get home about seven each morning, sleep until two in
the afternoon, then work on material for a comedy record album. Not that any record company wanted me to
do an album. My quitting Vegas had gotten around, and
nobody wanted me, not even for Bar Mitzvahs.
    Sometimes I got discouraged.
    "How's it going?" Amy said, greeting me one day as I
waited for her on the porch of her parents' house.
    "Bad," I mumbled.
    She sat down beside me.
    "Tell the coach about it."
    "Nothing's funny anymore."
    We took a walk. Amy tried to prime the funny pump.
"What do you see?"
    "A man mowing his lawn," I mumbled.
    "Why's that funny?"
    "It isn't."
    "C'mon, work with me." She tried again. "I under-
stand you're the world's greatest bird expert. How would
you describe yourself to our listeners?"
    She waited.
    "Cheap," I answered, almost as a reflex action.
    "Doctor, what kind of bird is that on the tree over
there?"
    "What tree?"
    "What do you mean? Can't you see that tree?"
    "That? I thought it was a giant rooster."
    "Seriously, doctor, is that a pheasant?"
    "It's a robin with ring around the collar."

She squeezed my hand and winked. "That's absurd, doctor."

I was feeling better. "No—we're too far west for a surd."

"Look up there. Is that an eagle?"

"That's a robin with a membership to a Jack La Lanne Health Club."

"Frankly, doctor, I seriously doubt your credentials. What would you call a penguin?"

"Harry. It seems to fit, doesn't it?"

"I don't mean that. If you saw a penguin one day, what would you think?"

"I'd missed a turn on the freeway?"

"In your book, what do you call a penguin?"

"A robin with a stuck zipper on his tux."

She started laughing. I'd made her laugh. I fell in love all over again.

I was a basket case without her. As a coach, she spent her whole life telling people they could achieve their goals. She believed it about everyone. She believed it about her tall, slender center who was so nervous and un-coordinated she'd fall down even when nobody was around her, until Amy kept asking her to think of a song and sing it to herself during the game and forget the crowd. She believed it about one of her players built like a tank, great on the basketball court, but no dates off-season until Amy worked with her on hair and complex-ion. And she believed it about me—that I'd succeed.

Her face was like a gentle sea breeze to me. She brought hope and goodness and calm and light.

My very own coach.

We entered a shopping center. I bought us hot dogs and root beer. We browsed. Watching people wash clothes in a Laundromat, she said, "Give me something about Laundromats."

"I love Laundromats. It's like a show-and-tell for

dirty clothes. The dryers at a Laundromat have two settings, damp and burnt. Another thing—you can find
magazines there you can't get anywhere else—like *Mod-
ern Werewolf,* or magazines with strange household hints,
like ten uses for toenail clippings."

We walked into a grocery store, past the dairy case.
She said, "Buttermilk."

"Have you ever known anyone who actually admitted
to liking buttermilk? You ever tasted buttermilk? You
know what it is? Sour milk. Every carton of regular milk
has a date stamped on it and you're not supposed to buy
it after the date stamped on the carton or it'll be bad. You
ever notice the dates on a carton of buttermilk? October
13, 2140. I mean, when everything that can possibly go
wrong with milk has happened, then they call it buttermilk."

"Cheese," she said.

"When I was a kid, people used to tell me the moon
was made of green cheese. I believed 'em, but I used to
imagine that, somewhere in the universe, there was a
giant cracker in orbit."

I grabbed her hand and we skipped through the mall
and nobody noticed. That's L.A. for you. We walked
home holding hands.

"You really get to me," she said.

"Tell me all about it, my dear." I rubbed my hands,
impersonating a melodrama villain out to get little Nell.

"When I'm with you, with all your joking and kidding, I feel like this is the Real World, and that everything else in my life is crazy. Like today in faculty meeting. We spent forty-five minutes trying to decide if we
should have a pop machine in the faculty lounge. You'd
have thought it was the United Nations. The worst part
was, everybody wanted it. It was a two-minute issue. But
no—somebody amends the original motion to strike out
the words 'Coke machine' and replace it with 'soda pop
machine.' Then we had amendments to amendments.

Somebody kept yelling 'Point of order!' It was insane. So I come home and we pretend that there's a giant cracker in orbit and that a woman on TV washes her face with a dove—and it all makes complete sense to me! Why does the real world seem absolutely bonkers to me?"

I grinned. "Because it is. That's what keeps comedians going—the real world is crazy."

She looked at me. "You know what? I'm hooked on you. Absolutely—your wit, your charm, your silly face."

I frowned. "Ms. Chairperson, I'd like to amend that by striking out the word *silly* and inserting the word *handsome.*"

In another accent, I said, "Point of order, point of order."

I continued for a while on that. It really cracked her up.

Amy's parents invited me for supper. Afterwards she and I sat out on her porch. I put my arm around her and started the timer and we kissed. The night breeze brought the smell of flowers to us from the garden. Moonlight softly lit her face.

Holding her in my arms, I whispered quietly, "I'll never forget the first girl I dated, Ima Frog. I picked her up at her house. She'd really gotten dressed up for the occasion—she put new shoelaces in her combat boots. I met her parents. Her mother was in the kitchen writing threatening Christmas cards."

She slugged me. "So help me, Jimmy Pepper, if you ruin a romantic mood like this on our honeymoon, you'll be in big trouble. I mean BIG TROUBLE."

We kissed until the timer went off; then she went inside for the night.

During the time of waiting to go to the temple so we could be married, and waiting to put together enough money to get my comedy album recorded, I got discouraged. One thing helped—Jill sent me information about my great-great-grandfather.

Archibald Pepper was born in Scotland. When he was thirteen years old, he was apprenticed to learn the shoemaking trade. He lived away from his parents in another town. When he was fifteen years old, he heard the missionaries preach. He believed what they said and wrote asking his parents for permission to be baptized. They said if he joined the church, he would never again be welcome in the family.

He was baptized. When he was eighteen, he crossed the Atlantic Ocean in the ship *Samuel Curling* and crossed the plains in Milo Andrus's company. He was separated from his parents when he was young—just like Jill and Ryan and me.

Once Jill sent me the minutes of several church meetings where he had spoken.

June 6, 1895. He told about leaving his homeland as a boy, about the hardships of traveling across the plains, about seeing women bury their husbands and children. At the time he gave the talk, he had been hunted for a year by federal officials pursuing him because of his having entered into plural marriage. He concluded his talk with these words: "We should be willing to make sacrifices for the gospel's sake."

My sacrifice was waiting so that Amy and I could be married worthily in the temple. Maybe it's not as great as crossing the plains, but to me it was a serious challenge.

November 3, 1895. The clerk recorded in his minutes: "Brother Pepper addressed the meeting, spoke of our meeting together and partaking of the sacrament, that we might have the Spirit of the Lord to be with us always that we should not have hard feelings one towards another, but we should have the holy spirit to be with us at all times."

Roots. I have a great-great-grandfather. He gave me a legacy, a lineage, a tradition to uphold.

He was a Mormon pioneer. Do you know what I'm saying? My very own pioneer ancestor.

We spend most of our life just trying to find out who we are. Once we know, we suddenly see that all of us, somewhere down the line, come from noble men and women.

During our engagement, Amy's team made it to the regional basketball tournament. I'd spent time with the team during practices, mainly just waiting for Amy to be finished. Gradually I got to know the members of the team. I'd sit in the empty stands, and they'd come over once in a while, and we'd sort of joke around.

They were an easy group to care about. Nice kids. Very competitive.

I got some of them using garlic.

They asked Amy if I could talk to them just before their first game at the tournament. She thought they'd have wanted the principal, but they wanted me.

After they were ready, Amy escorted me into the dressing room where the team waited, just a few minutes before the game was to begin. They were very nervous and tense.

I began. "First of all, I guess I don't need to tell you how important this game is. You've come a long way to get here—what was it, thirty miles? It wasn't easy getting here either. Mainly because your bus driver lost his way. I knew you were in trouble when he welcomed you to Disneyland. But you're here and that's the important thing."

A few looked up. It sounded almost like the usual before-game speech, but not quite.

"I guess I don't have to tell you this is the most important game of your life, not only to you individually, but to your high school. You will never in your entire life play a more important game. This is it. Don't blow it. If you lose this game, a scarlet tattoo will be placed on your forehead that will read, 'I lost regionals.' You will be forced to wear that for the rest of your life. Not only that, you will be sentenced to live alone in a small cottage outside a tiny village in New England, and tourists will come and pay a quarter to take pictures of you and your forehead standing alongside their nephew Melvin.

"If you lose, your principal and three shop teachers will slash their wrists in a rented hot tub in the parking lot of your high school. If you lose, four hundred unblemished navel oranges and three white Volkswagens will be burned at the stake. Also if you lose, your parents will receive threatening letters from Sesame Street. Mr. Rogers will phone you personally to say you're not special to him. McDonald's will shout in your ears that you don't deserve a break today. That's what'll happen if you lose today.

"But even so—don't be nervous."

One of the girls, named Patrimo, started giggling.

I continued. Pretty soon they were all laughing.

Finally it was time for them to go. Amy, with her clipboard, looked every bit the coach.

I wrapped it up. "Hey, we've had fun, but listen to me. You got an advantage now. The other team's going to be so tight, they'll squeak. Play loose. Enjoy yourselves. In the words of a famous Alpha Beta checkout lady, 'Have a nice day.' Now go out there and play ball! Let's do a cheer. Give me an E . . ."

"E!" they shouted.

"Give me an X!"

"X!"

"Give me a Q!"

"Q!"

"Give me a Z!"

"Z!"

"What does it spell?"

Giggles.

"Okay, so I don't know what it is, but you gotta admit it's a great word for Scrabble."

Laughter.

"Give me a car!"

"Car!"

"Thanks, I needed a car."

"Give me a wife!"

"Wife!"

"All right!" I grabbed Amy and kissed her, much to their delight and Amy's embarrassment. "Now go out there and destroy them!"

When the game started, Amy's team was so loose and the other team so nervous that our kids pulled out to an early ten-point lead.

Watching Amy during the game was good for me. Sometimes a guy gets to thinking of a woman as "my girl," almost as if she were a possession. But as I sat on the sidelines watching her—calling time-outs, bringing the team in for a little lesson on defense, sending them out again, sitting on the bench looking at the clock, wiping a wisp of hair from her eyes, standing up complaining about a bad call, bringing Patrimo out of the game for a few minutes to talk to her about what she was doing wrong, then hugging her before sending her back out again—I realized what a strong person Amy was. She would never be my shadow. I would never swallow her up, or cause her to lose her unique identity. We would share and give and assist and nurture, but she was Amy, and marriage wasn't going to change that.

We were so different from each other. I mean, here I was, about to marry a woman who had her own set of bar-bells. She could do forty pushups in a minute.

During the game there was a bad call. Amy threw her hands in the air and stood up to complain to the referee, her eyes flashing, her expression one of controlled anger.

She argued energetically but, of course, lost. Just as

the referee was about to call a technical, she sat down. I looked at her. She was in full control. The outburst had been staged for her players' benefit, to let them know she cared and to make the referee cautious the next time. I admired her. She was good at what she did.

We won 64 to 58.

I was the team mascot for the rest of the tournament, going with them to eat, spending the pregame time with them, telling jokes when Amy asked me to, warding off boys at night outside their motel rooms.

Two-thirty in the morning, the second night we were there, Amy and I stood guard in a hallway. Two guys had already tried to sneak into one of the girls' rooms— mainly because the girls invited them.

We sleepily leaned on each other in the hall.

She was worried. "The flu's going around, you know. What if somebody gets it? What if Patrimo gets it?"

"Patrimo won't get it," I said confidently.

"How do you know?"

"Patrimo's taking garlic. If garlic'll keep vampires away, it'll certainly stop the flu."

She relaxed. I kissed her.

I whispered in her ear. "Unless, of course, you're attacked by a vampire with the flu . . ."

She was in no mood for humor. "Who else is taking garlic?" she whispered.

"Sullivan."

I kissed an earlobe.

"Patrimo?" she whispered again.

"Patrimo and Sullivan."

She sighed contentedly. "Sullivan too."

"And Myers," I whispered softly in her ear.

She smiled. "I'm glad about Myers."

"Coach?"

"Yes," she said, content to be in my arms.

"I love you. Sometime tell me about b-ball, okay. Like what did you tell Patrimo during that time-out in the second half? You don't have to tell me now—I know you're tired, but sometime teach me about coaching. Okay?"

We kissed again, a slow, luxurious kiss; then she pulled away. "Time-out," she whispered, giving the appropriate signal.

I nodded in agreement. It was time to quit.

"Where will you sleep tonight?" she asked. All the rooms in the cheap motels were booked for the tournament.

"The YMCA. They're full but I'm gonna rent a racquetball court and four towels. If I can keep winning, I'll have a room."

She smiled. "You can't let a joke go by, can you." She started back down the hall. "It's too bad we're not married. My room is really nice."

I groaned. "C'mon, give me a break. Don't talk about your room."

We backed away from each other.

I blew her a kiss. "I've got to get out of here. Goodnight, Amy. I love you."

"Goodnight. Thanks for helping with the team. I appreciate you being so supportive."

She went to her room and closed the door.

I left for the YMCA and another cold shower. By this time in our engagement, I'd taken so many cold showers, I had a rash.

The team made it to the finals, where they lost by two points in the last five seconds. It was a heartbreaker.

I waited around in the hall outside the girls' dressing room after the game.

Amy came out to see me. "The girls want to see you. Can you come in?"

She escorted me in. The girls were just sitting there with their heads down, a couple of them crying.

"Hey, what's wrong with you guys?"

"We let everybody down," Patrimo said, wiping her eyes.

"You're wrong about that. You were terrific. You kept fighting back, even when you were down ten points. You wouldn't give up. Look, I love you guys. I've never been more proud of anybody."

I wiped my eyes.

"Look, anybody'd have trouble with the team you played tonight. Their center, for example. I'm not saying she was tall, but did you notice that she didn't stand at attention for the 'Star-Spangled Banner' until three minutes after the game started? And their other star, Wells, did you notice the coach plugged her into the wall during a time-out?"

In a few minutes they were laughing again.

Amy walked me out to the hall and explained how she had to go home on the bus, and how tired she was, and that she needed some time to catch up on her sleep, and that it might be a couple of days before she was ready to see me again.

I nodded. She kissed me on the forehead.

"You're a lamb," she said.

I nodded. "You notice how good I'm getting at waiting."

"It won't be much longer, you know. One more month and we'll be married in the temple."

I sighed. "It's just a matter of a little self-discipline, right?"

"Right, and you've been super. Just one thing, after we're married, can I wear perfume again?"

Three weeks before the wedding, just after coming back from picking up our announcements, I told Amy about my past.

"But you don't drink now, do you?"

"No, but once an alcoholic, always an alcoholic. I just

want you to know what you're getting yourself into. If I ever started drinking again, it'd be bad news for our family."

I thought she'd say it was all right, that she didn't care about what'd happened in the past, that what was important was I'd repented—but she didn't. She just sat there looking disappointed.

"How long has it been since you had a drink?" she asked.

"Good grief, Amy, do we have to go into every detail?"

"I think we do," she said quietly.

"All right then—it's been a year and a half."

She opened the car door to leave. "I need time to think, okay?"

Early the next day, which was Saturday, she came to my apartment, returned the engagement ring, quickly said it would be better if we broke up, then turned and left me.

I was alone all over again—I needed a drink.

I sat down, my head lowered, my eyes closed, mumbling prayer after prayer as sweat poured off me, fighting to stay in my apartment, willing myself to stay put and not go out for something to drink.

Fifteen minutes passed. It seemed like forever.

I pulled out my genealogy and read about my ancestors, reading aloud over and over the names and dates of birth and marriage and death. How old was he when he got married? How old was his wife? How many children did they have? Where was he born? How old was he when he got married? Where was he born? Over and over again.

I called my home teachers. They came and talked to me. They took me golfing. They kept me walking through eighteen holes. I'd never been golfing in my life. I was so terrible at it. But I got through the day. And at night one of them made me come home with him and help him put up a swing set for his kids, and stay for supper, and play Pac-Man on his Atari, and watch TV until late, and then sleep on his couch.

I got up early the next morning, went home, took a shower, and got ready for church. I arrived there two hours early and just sat in the chapel, where I was safe. I helped the custodian set up chairs for a Sunday School class. I read about the Garden of Gethsemane.

A few minutes before church began, Amy came over to me. "May I talk to you privately?"

We went into the cultural hall.

"How are you doing?" she asked.

"I'm sober. That's what counts."

She hugged me and started crying. My hands stayed at my side. We were alone in the center of the basketball court, and the congregation in the chapel was singing the opening song.

"My dad's outside in the car. He wants to talk to you."

I went out to see him. It was like the shootout at the OK Corral, with us facing each other in the middle of the parking lot.

"I talked Amy into breaking up with you as a test to see how strong you were. It was just a test."

"A test? You mean to see if I'd stay sober?"

He nodded. "I had to know. By the way, you passed."

I was furious. "You had no right to do that!"

"Probably not."

"With all due respect, sir, I think you're a blockhead."

He smiled grimly. "Probably—but someday you'll have a daughter too. Then I'll watch you become a blockhead too."

"So what am I supposed to do? Smile and say it's okay what you did to me, then go off and marry your daughter?"

"That's what you'll do if you have any sense. She loves you."

"A test!" I fumed. "Of all the stupid ideas! Playing

with my life for your amusement. If you just knew what you put me through yesterday."

"I know what I put you through," he said quietly.

We stared at each other.

"You do?"

"I know exactly what it was like. So does Amy. She was ten when I quit drinking."

I looked at him as if for the first time.

"So you see, I had to know. She's my daughter. I love her. I couldn't bear for her to go through what her mother went through. Some day you'll have a daughter, and you'll understand. Maybe you'll come up with a test of your own."

"Look, I want an apology," I said.

We stared at each other. "Okay, I'm sorry."

"You should be," I said bitterly.

He shrugged his shoulders and drove away.

I went inside. Amy was waiting for me.

"I'm sorry." She hugged me.

"Why did you do it?" I asked, still feeling betrayed.

"I don't know. My dad . . ."

"Don't listen to him anymore." I put my arms around her and held her close to me. "Amy," I whispered.

"What?"

"Nothing. I just like saying your name."

I held her and we kissed. It was a long kiss. It would have been longer, but we realized the door to the chapel was open, and people in the meeting were staring at us.

We were married in the Los Angeles Temple. Scott and Jill were there with us. The ceremony was sacred. Amy's parents waited outside for us; then there was a reception at the church.

Just before we left on our honeymoon, Scott and Jill walked with us to my car. Scott looked in where we had hung some clothes.

"You ironed your pajamas?" he asked, looking more closely at my clothes hanging from the rack.

I blushed. "Well, yes, I . . ."

He turned to Jill and chuckled. "He ironed his pajamas."

Jill smiled. "Yes, I see he did."

"Well," I stammered, "I often iron my pajamas."

Scott reached in and grabbed the pajamas from the hanger. "Hey, look what we got here!" he shouted.

"Gimme that!"

He sidestepped me and started waving them like a flag. "Look, everybody! Designer PJ's!"

I grabbed them away. Trying to salvage some dignity, I said, "Amy, it's time to go now."

"I never saw designer PJ's before," Scott said. "Jill, did you see the little designer insignia sewn on the back?"

"Goodbye, we're leaving now," I said quickly.

Jill and Amy hugged each other. Scott and I shook hands. He was still grinning like an idiot about my pajamas.

We waved goodbye and drove off—just the two of us, to enjoy our best wedding presents—each other.

Shortly after we were married, I recorded my comedy album. The next job was trying to sell them. I'd take them to music stores and they'd take a few on consignment.

Amy became pregnant four months after we were married. The room that was to be the baby's was stacked with copies of my record album.

I went to radio stations to beg them to play segments from the album. Out of ten stations, two agreed to play it. I even tried selling the records door to door, sort of an Avon Man for comedy.

". . . Now here's Johnny!"

I sat in a room with the other guests. They were all drinking to relax. I went into the bathroom and prayed.

One of the guests had been on the show several times. "Can you tell me what Johnny's really like?" I asked.

He shrugged. "I don't know him that well."

"How about some advice then?"

"Just be yourself," he said, finishing his drink.

"Do I have a choice? Who else can I be?"

"Exactly," he said. "Who else?"

It was a fluke about being invited to appear on the show. The niece of a staff member for Carson bought one of the albums and sent it to her aunt for a gift. The aunt played it the same day and asked her husband to listen to it. After he heard it, he made a mental note to find out more about me, but forgot until one of the regular guests came down with the flu. The staff person suggested me, and the next day he brought the album to work. Carson listened to about three minutes and said for them to get me. A day later I was contacted and asked to come the next day and do one of the routines that was on the record.

That's how I got there that night. I am one of the few people in the world grateful for the flu.

I got a glass of water and had a couple of garlic pills.

"Uppers?" one of the guests asked.

"Garlic," I said.

"Italian?" he asked hopefully.

"Scottish."

"A scotch sounds good to me," another guest said, her voice becoming slurred.

Fifteen minutes before the end of the show, I went on.

"Would you please welcome an up-and-coming new comic, Jimmy Pepper!"

Please, have a sense of humor, I prayed, walking on stage.

The rest is history.

My agent was kept busy the next week.

CHAPTER NINE

We reached Buffalo, Wyoming, about seven at night. After stopping to get directions at a gas station, we found the trailer court. It was on the edge of town. Hank's trailer was old, with some paint beginning to wear off. (I'd given up any hope of calling him Dad.) There was a note on the door telling us that he was at work. He gave us directions and promised us a free car wash if we'd go see him.

It was a coin-operated car wash with eight bays. Hank was in an office the size of a closet listening to a customer complain about losing his money in one of the machines.

"You just can't let the quarter roll in," Hank said. "You gotta push it in. Otherwise it doesn't trigger the mechanism."

"It says insert four quarters. If you gotta throw 'em in, you oughta change your instruction list. Anyway, I put the money in and nothing happened."

Hank walked with him back to his bay to get the machine started.

A few minutes later Hank returned. A shapely coed with a University of Wyoming T-shirt complained that the dollar changer wouldn't take her dollar. Hank turned the dollar bill over and pushed it into the machine. Out came four quarters. She left.

A cattle truck started to pull in the truck bay. Hank rushed after it, shouting. "Hey! You guys are clogging my drains! Take a shovel and clean all that out before you turn on the water! See that barrel? Put it in there."

He returned to us, still watching the guy in the cattle

truck to make sure he got all the manure cleaned out before he turned on the water.

"Cattle trucks," he muttered, then turned to face us.

"Daddy!" Jill cried out, throwing her arms around him.

He was shorter than me, and wore a baseball cap and a long-sleeved gray work shirt and slacks. His face was lean, almost gaunt, yet very tan.

We awkwardly shook hands. "How's it going?" I asked.

"Can't complain. How about you? How was your trip?"

"Fine," I said.

Jill told him about the man from the *National Inquirer*. "Why didn't you talk to him?"

I answered. "He wants to do a story about when I was growing up."

"You're afraid he'll find out about me?"

"Well, I . . ."

He left to take care of a customer. We waited in the office for him. There were a pile of magazines and several coffee cups and a tool chest and one chair and an old radio tuned to a country music station. Jill sat on the stool and I leaned against the wall.

"Well," Hank said, returning after helping someone. "It's been a long time."

"Sure has," Jill said.

"A long time," I echoed.

A man appeared at the door. "Excuse me. I need some advice. We're tourists, see, and about twenty minutes ago our youngest kid threw up all over the back seat. I thought I'd take off the kid's clothes and spray 'em down, and maybe wash him off too. So my question is, what'd be the best setting for my kid—Wash, Rinse, or Wax?"

We looked at him.

"Well, for a little kid, I don't think I'd use Wax," Hank said.

"Okay," the man said.

"And I think Wash might be too hot for him. Is it a boy?"

"Yeah."

"I'd say Rinse'd be the best."

"Appreciate it," the man said.

The man pulled into the first stall.

"No! Don't!" a boy shouted. He cried through the whole cycle.

"You meet all kinds here," Hank said.

At ten he closed his office. We followed him home.

Five bags of trash were piled outside his door, evidence he'd worked hard cleaning up the place for us. It was a small trailer with faded linoleum floors and a small black-and-white TV. A couch facing the TV was covered with a large horse blanket to hide the damage to the fabric. In the winter he must have taped clear plastic sheets over the windows to keep the cold out. It was still there on all but two of the windows. Propped next to one window was a large fan, which he turned on as soon as we entered.

"Well, this is home. It's not much, but it's mine."

"It's fine," Jill said.

"Sure is," I repeated.

He opened the refrigerator and pulled out a bucket of Kentucky Fried Chicken, a container of coleslaw, and some doughy white rolls.

"How about this for supper?" he said proudly. "Finger licking good—right?"

"You bet!" I said, sounding too enthusiastic. Either I was very nervous or else I was an actor in a chicken commercial.

"I thought about what I could get to eat, and all of a sudden it hit me. Everybody likes Kentucky Fried Chicken. You want regular or extra crispy?"

"Doesn't matter to me," I said, thinking if I said crispy he'd only have regular. No use rocking the boat.

"Me either," Jill said.

"You can have either one. I got both. What'll it be?"

"Crispy," I said quickly.

"Regular," Jill said.

"Right—one crispy, one regular." He rummaged through the bucket. "Now, let's see, you want a leg, a thigh, or a breast piece?"

"It doesn't matter, Hank," I said.

"Suit yourself," he said. "Have whatever you want. I got legs, thighs, wings, and breasts."

"Well, a leg'd sure be great!" I said, sounding hyper.

"You're sure that's what you want?"

"A leg, sure, a leg'd be great! Boy, it's been a long time since I've had some of the Colonel's chicken! Yessir."

He rummaged through the bucket. "Let's see now, I forgot, you want a regular leg or an extra crispy leg?"

"Extra crispy. Let's go all the way, shall we?" I actually chuckled.

He handed me a leg, and I sat and held it. He had not yet put out plates.

I'd never felt more uncomfortable in my life.

"Jill?"

"A regular wing," she said.

He rummaged through the bucket and then swore. "Wouldn't you know it? Look at that wouldya? I don't got wings in regular. I told the girl too. 'One of each,' I said. But would you look at that—two crispy wings. I should've checked it before I left the store."

"It really doesn't matter," she said.

"No, no—we'll get you what you want. If you want a wing, you can have a wing, but it'll be crispy, or if you want crispy, we got crispy legs, and crispy thighs, and . . ."

"Daddy, I don't really care that much what I have."

". . . or if you'd rather, I'll go back and get you a regular wing. It's just down the street. It was their fault anyway."

"No, really, whatever you've got will be fine," she said.
"You sure?"

"Really, it doesn't make any difference."

"If you're sure." He handed her a crispy leg. "Here
you go." He looked around. "Now then—everybody
fixed up for chicken? Okay. You know, when I picked it
up, I had a choice. I could've got gravy or coleslaw. I decided in the summer nobody wants gravy, so I got the
coleslaw. Is that all right with everyone? I guess we could
go back and get gravy too, if you want. Chicken gravy's
nice sometimes."

"Coleslaw'll be fine," Jill said.

"Actually, I prefer coleslaw to gravy," I echoed.

"You know, me too," he said, dishing up some coleslaw on paper plates. "Must run in the family. Okay,
here's your plate of coleslaw. Now, what would you like
to drink? I got beer, but I guess you don't want that, do
you. That'll be for me. Pepsi, orange soda, Seven-up,
orange juice, root beer, and Coke, and, oh yeah, I almost
forgot, milk—fresh milk. Got it today. So what'll it be?"

I'd had it. "Are we gonna talk like this all night? It's
like living in a TV commercial."

He misunderstood, scowled, stormed to the refrigerator, and pulled out a can of beer for himself, a half
gallon of milk, and several cans of soda pop.

"Take what you want," he muttered.

We sat and ate and watched small screen black-and-
white TV. TV is wonderful when you don't really want to
talk. It gives the appearance of togetherness. After an
hour, I had a huge pile of bones on my plate. It was the
only thing I could think of doing.

Hank turned off the TV because a presidential news
conference was on and it was covered by both stations.

I felt as if someone had taken away my life raft. There
was just the three of us together in a small trailer. We
would have to say something.

Jill saved me. "Daddy, would you like to see some pictures of your grandchildren?" She handed him a stack of photos. He started through them. "Who's he?" he asked.

"My husband."

"What's his name?"

"Scott."

"Going bald, isn't he?"

She smiled good-naturedly. "We joke about it sometimes."

She leaned over the pictures with him. "The oldest here is Kirk, and our baby is Justen."

"Justen? What kind of a name is that?"

"It was Scott's father's middle name. He's been very helpful."

The sentence dangled in midair. He finished the stack of pictures and turned to me.

"You got any?"

I handed him some pictures from my wallet.

"This your wife?" he asked.

I nodded. "Her name is Amy."

He chuckled. "She's a tall one, isn't she."

"What of it?" I said with just the hint of an edge to my voice.

"Nothing—don't get excited. I just noticed she's tall. If she was short, I'd have said, 'Short, isn't she.' Don't be so touchy."

"She used to be a high school girls' basketball coach. Now she coaches girls' softball during the summer."

He studied the picture. "Taller than you?"

"No," I snapped.

"Close though, I bet."

"What difference does it make?"

"None at all."

He looked at a picture of our baby. "What's his name?"

"Logan."

He paused. "You named your kid after a town?"

"It was the name of my foster father."

It was the wrong thing to say. He quickly laid the picture down. "Well now, we'd better get these things in the refrigerator, and then we gotta figure out sleeping arrangements for tonight. There's only one bed. Jill, you can have that. Jimmy can take the couch here, and I got an air mattress. I'll just put it down on the floor with a sleeping bag."

"We can't let you sleep on the floor," Jill said. "Let me use the sleeping bag."

"No, it'll be fine."

We made arrangements for the bathroom. Jill would be first, me second, and Hank third.

He turned on the TV.

When I came out of the bathroom, Hank went in.

I sat down on the couch near Jill.

"Well?" she asked.

"It was our duty to see him, and we have. But there's no reason to drag it out. When's the soonest we can get out of here? How about tomorrow morning?"

Hank came out of the bathroom. "Guess what I got planned for us tomorrow?" he said brightly. "I'm taking a few days off. I thought we'd go camping. As long as you've come this far, you ought to see the Bighorns. There's a wilderness area you've just got to see."

"What's a wilderness area?"

"Except for a few trails they've built, they've pretty much left things the way they were before the white man."

"Why would they want to do that?" I asked.

"We'll have to hike a few miles. We're going to the Seven Brothers Lakes. I got us backpacks and everything we'll need. Sounds fun, don't it, just the three of us?"

"I have to get back to California," I said.

"Get back? Already?"

Jill looked at me, questioning me with her expression. I finally nodded. "We'll go camping," Jill said.

He turned on TV to Johnny Carson. Jill said goodnight and went to bed.

"What's Johnny Carson really like?" he asked.

"I don't know. The only time I was with him was when
we were on the air. You know him as well as I do."

"I thought maybe you would've gone out for pizza
with him after the show."

"No."

"Well, did he say anything to you after the show?"

"Yes, he said, 'Hey, great to have you.'"

We watched a few more minutes.

"What's Ed McMahon really like?"

"Hank, I just don't know."

"Hank," he muttered, then turned off the TV and
rolled out his sleeping bag, blew up his air mattress, and
lay down.

"Oh, one thing," he said. "I hope you get to sleep before I do, because people say I snore pretty bad."

I tried to concentrate on going to sleep. It didn't
work. Before long, he was asleep and snoring. Sometimes his cigarette cough would wake him up, and he'd
quit snoring for a while.

Snoring and coughing and breathing.

I tried to imagine what it'd sound like in a tent.

We got up the next morning and packed. Hank had
bought two new packs and sleeping bags and ponchos
and fishing outfits just for us.

By ten-thirty we were ready to go. As I stepped outside to load Jill's pack in the pickup, I noticed the *National
Inquirer* photographer's car across the street. He was taking pictures of us. As we left town he tailed us as we drove
into the Bighorns.

We turned off the highway and followed a narrower
road till it ended at a corral. Ahead of us was a bumpy,

boulder-strewn road fit only for vehicles with high clearance.

We parked and stepped out of the car. The photographer, Becker, pulled up beside us and got out.

"Get out of here!" I shouted.

Hank looked at me strangely.

"He's the one from the *National Inquirer*."

"You're from the *National Inquirer*?" Hank asked.

"That's right."

"I read it all the time." He shook Becker's hand.

Becker relaxed. "Terrific. We're doing a little article about your son."

"Jimmy's been on Johnny Carson. Did you know that?"

"Yes, sir."

"We're real proud of him. Well, you'd like to take some pictures of us."

"I don't want him taking pictures!" I snapped.

"Nonsense. He came all this way."

"Mr. Pepper, is it true you spent time in a Mexican prison?"

"He doesn't have to answer that!" I shouted. "C'mon, let's go. Don't talk to him, Hank."

"Why are you calling your father Hank?" Becker asked.

"Because that's his name. C'mon, let's go if we're going!"

I started almost pushing Hank ahead of me. Suddenly he stopped, pulled my hand off his shoulder, and turned to confront me. "Are you that ashamed of me?"

Then he walked back to Becker. "Yeah, I did time in prison. It's not something I'm proud of, but it happened. You'll have to forgive Jimmy. He's still bitter."

The two of them talked for a few minutes. Becker asked if he could get a picture of the three of us together before he left. Hank said yes.

"Jimmy, can I get you to move a little closer to your father?"

Grudgingly I moved in. "Becker, what kind of story are you going to write?"

"A good one, I bet," Hank said. "You think Jimmy'll be on the cover?"

"Maybe—you never can tell."

Becker left, and we started our hike.

"Who knows what he'll write," I complained to Jill as we struggled up the bumpy, rock-strewn road.

"Maybe just the truth," she said.

"I hope not," I said.

Half an hour later my back and legs were killing me. "Are we almost there?" I asked Hank.

"Oh, no. We got seven more miles to go."

It was terrible. Hank kept saying how beautiful the scenery was, but I never had enough energy to look up. All I saw were rocks.

You ordinarily think a lake would be in a valley. Not these lakes. The Seven Brothers Lakes are on top of a mountain that is surrounded by even higher peaks. The last mile to the lake is murder—up a switchback trail.

Finally we reached the top. I collapsed on the ground, panting. But we were there. We'd made it. I could see the lake just off the trail.

"Well, let's get going again," Hank said after a few minutes.

"Go?" I gasped. "We're already on top of the world."

"Most people stop at the first lake and fish. But the really good fishing is at the seventh lake. It's only another mile."

We started along the trail again. "Shoot me, Jill," I mumbled as we stumbled after Hank.

Finally we arrived at the seventh lake and picked out a camping site. There were no other humans in sight.

It was Hank's show. He set up the tent, fixed our

fishing poles, even baited our hooks, and showed us how to cast out. We had a small red bobber placed a foot from the hook and worm. Our job was to watch our bobber and wait for it to dip down when a fish bit.

"Hey, you kids remember when I took you fishing one time? It was when we were on a vacation to Glacier National Park. Jimmy was, let's see, I don't know, must've been six or seven. You remember?"

"Oh?" Jill said with a puzzled expression on her face.

"Remember we rented a little boat. It was just the three of us. Your mother wasn't feeling well. She stayed in the cabin. Just the three of us. Ryan would've been too young to go with us. Just the two big kids went fishing with Daddy. Remember now?"

We smiled weakly. Finally Jill lied. "I think I remember—just a little."

"Me too, just a little," I echoed.

He left to fix lunch.

"Is this supposed to be fun?" I complained as I tried to thread a worm on my hook.

"They say it is," she said.

"I wish there was a phone around here. I bet my agent is pulling his hair out, trying to get in touch with me. I've got an offer to do a movie, and another record, and maybe even some Las Vegas engagements. And what am I doing? Sitting on a log torturing worms. Suppose we do catch a fish, what's the market value? A buck? And another thing, someday we're going to have to hike back. Think about that."

Half an hour later Hank called us for a late lunch. He'd fried us some hamburgers over a campfire. He had everything fixed for us. All we had to do was eat and repeat over and over, "Boy, this is really great!"

"It really is, Daddy," Jill said.

"Nothing special," he replied.

"I guess it's just that food always tastes better outdoors," I said, trying to sound cheerful while carefully picking pine needles from my hamburger.

"Lookie here, what we got for dessert," he bubbled as he pulled out a package of marshmallows. "On that fishing trip, one night we had a campfire and roasted marshmallows. Jimmy kept setting his on fire. Jill, you remember how I spent ten minutes roasting one for you, golden brown? After that we all called you Goldie Brown. Remember? Now here's some sticks for you both to do your own."

I speared a marshmallow with my stick and stuck it in the fire. It caught on fire.

Hank laughed. "Hey, look at that, would you! Just like when you were a kid."

He watched with delight as I ate it. It tasted like soot.

Of course, Jill had to prepare one that was golden brown, and we all had to remark how times hadn't changed at all.

"Well, this sure brings back memories!" I said, trying to sound enthusiastic.

"Sure does, but don't stop now," he chuckled. "Have another one."

I just couldn't. "No thanks. They're so filling. One marshmallow really fills a fella up."

"There's plenty—I brought two packages."

The moment of truth had arrived. "Actually I guess I don't like 'em that much, not as much as I did when I was a kid."

"Jill?"

She shook her head. "No thanks . . . maybe later. I have to watch my weight all the time now."

It was painful seeing him there awkwardly holding two full bags of marshmallows. He looked disappointed. Finally he threw the marshmallows in the fire, and we sat and watched them burn.

"I'll just get the pans cleaned up," he said quickly. "You two go fish some more."

"Daddy," Jill said, "you don't have to do everything. We can help."

"No, no, this is your trip. You don't have to do a thing.

I'll do it all. Go fishing or take a walk, whatever you want. Just have a nice time."

We walked down by the lake while he cleaned up.

I swatted at a mosquito. Its remains were red with my blood. "You got any more mosquito repellent?"

"What do you mean, any more? I never had any to begin with."

"Let's get out of here. You game? We'll make a break for it tonight while the guards are sleeping."

She smiled but only a little. She wasn't as eager to get into fantasy as Amy.

A minute later she slapped my face.

"Ow!" I cried out.

"There was a mosquito on your face."

I rubbed my cheek where she'd hit me.

"Don't tell me—you missed it."

"Yeah, sorry."

I checked my bobber. No action. The fish were all taking naps.

There were a million flies buzzing around us. "I gotta get out of this place."

"Maybe we could go swimming," she suggested.

I put my hand in the water. It was ice cold because it was fed from snowdrifts.

"Whataya bet he reads bedtime stories to us tonight," I said.

We looked back. He was busily scouring out the frying pan.

A few minutes later I asked, "Where's the bathroom?"

"This is a wilderness area, remember."

I looked around desperately. "Not even an outhouse?"

"Nothing."

I panicked. "What are we supposed to do?"

"Find a nice fallen tree to sit on," she said.

I slapped at a mosquito. "People talk about getting

back to the basics, but let me tell you something—there's such a thing as too basic."

I took a lonely excursion into the woods to find a fallen tree. When I came back, she smiled. "Well?"

"Good grief," I mumbled disgustedly.

She suggested we take a walk along the path around the seventh lake. It was better than fishing, and the path was nearly level, so I agreed.

Part of the seventh lake looks almost as if it's at the bottom of a crater, because it's bounded by high mountain peaks. We found a waterfall fed from snow melting higher up. I'd brought a small cup with me, and we had a drink. It tasted good.

"Jimmy, we need to talk," she said.

We found a huge boulder that jutted out into the water and sat down on it to rest.

"So?"

"Tell me how you feel about Daddy."

"Good grief, how am I supposed to feel? He was the all-time world's worst father, and now he thinks he can barge into our lives and somehow make everything right, and we're all supposed to pretend the past doesn't exist."

"He has to try. We're all he's got."

"Don't give me that. And what about you? How come you can just walk in and kiss him hello after all this time and not miss a beat?"

She pursed her lips. "I love him."

I grumbled.

"I think you're having such a hard time because you were always Daddy's boy. I remember you sitting in that old junk car and playing truck driver by the hour."

"I don't remember that."

"Jimmy, what do you remember?"

"I remember he always had a six-pack in the refrigerator, and I remember he brought that woman into our house after Mom died."

"And you can't forgive him?"

"Why should I forgive him?"

"How can you expect to be forgiven of your mistakes when you can't forgive others?"

"I can forgive others. It's just him I can't forgive."

"How about giving me three good memories of Daddy," she said.

"What is this, Psychoanalyst for a Day?"

"I'm just saying there must have been some good memories too. Give me three. Take your time. I'm going to walk down to that cove and look around."

She left.

Three good memories.

He was never around, but when he was, he was magic. He'd take the three of us downtown to a toy store and let us pick out anything we wanted. One day he bought us three new bikes and one for himself, and we went to a store and bought a bunch of good things to eat—bologna and potato chips and pickles and olives and Twinkies and root beer and cookies. Then we went home and, without Mom's help, formed an assembly line and made sandwiches and put 'em in a pack sack and took off on our bikes. All we did was go to a park, but it all seemed a grand adventure—because he was there. And we ate our lunches on top of a slippery slide, and just for the fun of it, we let our garbage go down the slide, and Ryan thought it was so funny. Every time we did it he just cracked up, and we all giggled until our sides ached.

That's number one.

When we came home from Mom's funeral, he had us sit down on the couch in the living room and he told us Mom wasn't in the casket, she was in heaven, and we should never forget that, and not think of her as dead. She was happy where she was. Sometime we'd see her again.

Later that night I woke up and heard a sound coming from their bedroom. I tiptoed closer and looked through the half-open door and there he was, sitting on the bed, packing her clothes into a box. He looked so lonely. I went in to him and hugged him, and he held me and said it was going to be all right.

He asked me to help. With each dress, he told me a memory of her. There was the dress she was married in, and the dress she bought just to wear to a second-grade class program where I was going to recite a poem. "Old King Cole was a merry old soul, a merry old soul was he . . ." There was a black slip and a blue silk negligee I discovered in a drawer. He took them from me and quickly, almost roughly, shoved them into the box without a word.

We packed everything. Then he walked out of the room and shut the door tightly behind him and lay down on the couch in the living room. I sensed the terror of that night for him, and got my sleeping bag, and returned to sleep on the floor beside the couch, where he lay staring at the ceiling.

That's number two.

The third memory reached way back. It was of a five-year-old boy being boosted up into the cab of Daddy's semitruck. He and I sat up there, and he showed me how everything worked, and then I got to go out for a drive on the highway with Daddy in his big truck. We sat above all the other cars and trucks. It was like being a king of the road.

I was so proud my daddy was king of the road.

That's number three.

Jill came back. "Did you think of three good memories?"

"Yes."

"Want to tell me what they are?"

"Not now," I said soberly. "How about you?"

"He called me Princess," she said. "He always called me Princess, and that's the way he made me feel, like a princess."

"One time when we were kids," she said as we walked

back down the trail, "we all went to Primary and we
learned a song, and you said we were going to sing it for
Daddy when he came back from his trip. You made us
practice it every day, even Ryan, who couldn't have been
more than four or five years old. When Daddy came
back, we ran to him and you started us. We all sang, but
Ryan was always about ten seconds behind the rest of us.
I remember the song."

She sang it.

> *I'm so glad when Daddy comes home,*
> *Glad as I can be;*
> *Clap my hands and shout for joy,*
> *Then climb upon his knee;*
> *Put my arms around his neck,*
> *Hug him tight like this;*
> *Pat his cheeks, then give him What?*
> *A great big kiss.*

"You loved him once," she said.
"Maybe I did—once."
We started back.
"The memories don't change anything," I said. "He
still left us."
"I've heard you talk about great-great-grandfather
Archibald, about what a great man he was. What are you
going to do—glory in the dead ancestors you never knew
and dump on the one that's alive and you know best?"
We returned to camp. Hank was fishing. We sat down
with him. Suddenly his pole dipped down sharply and
the line started feeding out.
"I got one!" he yelled.
He fought against the fish. He kept reeling in, but
when the fish pulled too hard, the automatic drag allowed the line to feed out rather than break the line.
The trout jumped out of the water.
After a few minutes the fish tired out. Hank reeled it
in and dragged it onto the shore.

"Would you look at that?" Hank said proudly.

I picked up a large rock and knelt down to kill it so it wouldn't suffer.

"No! Let it go! Put it back in the water!" he said.

I grabbed the fish by the gills. The hook was deep inside the fish's mouth.

"I can't get it out."

"Hurry up then and cut the line!"

The trout twisted violently in my hands. Jill took a knife and cut the line, and the fish twisted away, fell into the water, and shot away. Not until it was gone did I realize that she'd cut the line on the wrong side of the red bobber. The fish had taken it along into the lake.

"What a fish!" Hank said in awe.

After that there seemed no point to continue fishing. We returned to camp.

Clouds started to roll in overhead. Hank set up the one-burner stove while Jill opened two packages of dried soup.

It started to rain.

We withdrew into the tent to get out of the rain. Jill climbed into her sleeping bag to stay warm. A few minutes later we brought the food in the tent and ate.

"This won't last," Hank said. "In Wyoming, they say if you don't like the weather, just wait five minutes and it'll change."

We listened to the steady patter of rain on our tent.

"Actually the fishing's best when it's raining. Maybe I'll go out and try it. Anyone want to come along?"

We shook our heads.

He went outside to get his fishing rod. A minute later, he opened the flap and looked in. "Where's my bobber?"

"When Jill cut the line, she cut on the wrong side. I guess the fish took it with him."

"My fish is dragging a bobber around with him?"

"Maybe it's come off by now," I said.

"Do you know how much that's gonna hurt when he goes down deep?"

"I'm sorry, Daddy," Jill said.

"Maybe I can cast out and snag the bobber and take it off."

Jill and I sat in the growing darkness and listened to the rain fall on the tent. We could hear him casting out time and time again and reeling in.

"Get him back before he catches pneumonia," Jill said.

I put on my poncho and ran down to him. The dull gray clouds now covered the entire sky. He stood alone in the rain, his baseball cap dripping, his fingers starting to get clumsy from the cold water. It was hopeless to try to cast out and hook the bobber and reel the fish back in. Why didn't he know it was hopeless?

"There he is." The red bobber moved steadily along the surface. He cast out toward the bobber but missed.

"Hank, we need to get back in or we'll catch a cold."

He watched the bobber move away from us.

"I'm just trying to help. I guess he don't know that."

"Give it up. He'll be all right."

We returned to the tent. His shirt and slacks were soaked.

"Daddy," Jill said, "take off your wet things and get in your sleeping bag."

He did neither. Instead he sat down on his sleeping bag and lit up a cigarette and worried about the fish.

I took off my wet sweatshirt and slacks and crawled into my sleeping bag.

"Daddy," Jill said, "you've got to get out of your wet things."

"Everytime he tries to eat, everytime he swallows, the hook'll be there, tearing away at him, hurting him."

"Will you shut up about that stupid fish?" I snapped.

"Jimmy," Jill cautioned.

I blew up. "You spend more time worrying about some dumb fish than you've ever spent on us. Why don't you ever ask about Ryan? He's dead. Why don't you care about him? Why don't you ever ask what he was like? And what about Jill? Not even a crummy birthday card for her all those years! And you worry about a fish! And what about me? I wasted half my life because of you! You're a fool to think that roasting marshmallows is going to make it all better! Let me tell you something, it won't. Nothing on earth will do that."

I quit.

He sat still, his expression frozen in time.

Half an hour later Jill finally talked him into getting out of his wet clothes and into his sleeping bag. We lay there in the tent, silently listening to each other breathe and the rain falling on the tent. Side by side, in the darkness of night, each sensing the icy presence of the others, each pretending to be asleep. It was the worst of tortures. My stomach tied itself into knots. But eventually I fell asleep.

The next thing I remember was Jill touching me on my head. "Jimmy, he's gone."

I sat up.

"What's wrong?" I said sleepily.

"He left the tent a minute ago. Go find out where he's gone. I'm worried."

The tent was pitch-black, and he'd taken the only flashlight. I rummaged around for my jeans and shoes and got dressed, then stepped outside.

It had quit raining. He was standing by the side of the lake. He shone the flashlight over the surface and then stopped. He'd seen the bobber. It was moving slowly.

I walked carefully from one large granite boulder to the next, trying to get out to where he was.

"Be careful," I warned.

I took a step—and fell in. The water was so cold I couldn't even yell.

A second later he was in the water with me, trying to save me.

"Leave me alone!" I said.

"Let me help you!"

"I don't need your help!"

We pulled and pushed each other up onto dry land.

After we got out of our wet things, we sat around the fire to warm up.

"How do you feel now?" Jill asked Hank.

He shrugged his shoulders. "Takes more than a little water to hurt a Pepper."

He made himself a cup of coffee and had a cigarette. Jill and I had hot chocolate.

With his head down, not looking at us, he started to talk. "After I moved back to Wyoming, I took up fishing on my days off. At first it was just something to do. But once I saw a man and his boy up here fishing. The kid had freckles and a baseball cap and tennis shoes. After a while the man got mad because his kid got the fishing line all messed up—looked just like a bird's nest. He had to untangle it for his kid."

He stopped.

When he started again, he spoke with a strange hoarseness to his voice. "I watched 'em together, just a man and his boy. Nothing special really, but I'd have given anything to have my kid mess up his fishing line for me to fix."

He didn't look at me. He looked into the fire. He couldn't look at me.

"After that I came up here a lot, I guess, in the back of my mind thinking someday I'd bring my kids, or maybe even my grandkids, here. But it's not the same. Time's passed me by. When I should've been with you, I wasn't."

He took a long draw on his cigarette. "There's nothing anybody can do to bring time back. It's just gone."

He tossed the cigarette in the fire.

"It was a dumb idea to bring the two of you up here."

Jill sat beside him and hugged him and told him she loved him.

But I didn't budge. Not me. Stone-faced, staring at dead ashes.

"The fire's down," he said. "I'll go get some more wood." He walked away.

Jill looked at me. "You know he's hurting."

"I know."

"Then help him."

"What can I do?"

"Tell him you love him."

Miserably I whispered, "I can't do that."

He brought back a log and laid it in the fire. He finally looked at me. "You think I didn't want to see you two after I got out? I did—you'll never know how much. But I was sure you'd both hate me, and I was too afraid to find out."

His face, reflected by the wavering flames, was full of shadows and light, tortured, old, and lonely.

He continued. "What I did was wrong. I know that. But you don't know what it was like for me when your mother died. You don't know what she was to me. She was the one who knew what was right. Without her, I was lost. After she died, I fell apart for a while. They said all I had to do was to go to Mexico and pick up a small package. They paid me five thousand dollars every trip. I was going to buy a ranch, and our family'd live there. I just needed to make a few more trips, and I'd be able to make a down payment on the place I wanted. But I was caught, and that was the end of that.

"When I got out of prison, the social workers in Cheyenne told me the three of you had gone to Idaho to live. I hitchhiked there. I talked to some people. They told me about Ryan. It was years after it'd happened. I went to Burley. They said Jimmy'd gone to California. Jill, I went to where you and your husband were living. I walked by the place and saw you there in the garden with your kid, maybe a year old, near you in a baby swing. I hid by a tree all afternoon watching the house. I guess I fell asleep, because when I woke up, I heard you saying to your kid, 'Grampa's coming!' Your kid started laughing. 'Grampa! Grampa!' you said over and over again. I couldn't believe my ears. I stood up, just about to walk into the yard, feeling like a new man. Then I saw a man get out of his car, a man with gray hair and a suit. He bent over and picked up your kid and kissed him, and then you all went inside, and I heard you ask if he wanted some lemonade, and then you shut the door. Your kid already had a grampa, a man who drove a nice car and wore suits. And what was I? A bum. I hitchhiked to Wyoming the same day."

"Daddy, oh, Daddy." She put her arm around his shoulder. "There was nothing in the whole world I wanted more than to see you again. Didn't you know that?"

"No."

He'd said his piece. It was all he'd say to try to mend things. Jill had managed it, but not me. It was my last chance.

He took one last sip of coffee and stood up, grabbed the flashlight, and walked into the darkness.

"Jimmy, please," Jill pleaded.

I shook my head. "I can't. I just can't."

She shook her head and stepped inside the tent to get ready for bed.

I stayed by the fire and waited for him to come back.

I was no longer a fifteen-year-old boy seeing the world in harshly drawn outlines. I've made mistakes in my life, but at least for every one, I can point to reasons why it happened. I'm willing to pay the price for my mistakes as long as someone understands there were underlying reasons.

There are reasons for me. And there were reasons for him.

Take Amy from me and what would I do? He did the best he could.

He returned to the campfire and glanced quickly at me, then turned away. "It's getting late. We'd better turn in. If you want, we can pack up and leave tomorrow. I know you got important things to do in California."

"Dad?"

It was the first time in eleven years I'd called him that.

"Yeah?"

I wanted to say that I knew it was hard when Mom died, and that it was hard for us to talk because we were so much alike, and that I'd made some mistakes in my life too but I'd found the Church, and it was important to me, and that he could do the same thing and go to the temple and have his marriage continue even after death so he could be with Mom someday, and that even Ryan, as good as he was, had had to repent, but then he moved beyond his mistakes, and how great a man he was at nineteen, and how much God must have needed him to take him so young, and about my little sister Jill, my little shepherd, how much I loved her, how important she'd been in my life. And I wanted to tell him about Amy, that when I was around her, everything was better. And about my son, still so small, and how it was to hold him and know I was his father, and that he needed me. I wanted to tell him that the past isn't as important as what we do from now on.

You were my hero. You were what men are supposed to be. You were what I wanted to become. Why did you leave me when all I wanted in life was to be like you, my dad, my king of the road?

King of the road.

King of the road.

My dad was king of the road.

There were layers to it that needed to be folded back, layers of feelings hidden for so long that needed to be exposed to sunshine.

There were so many things to tell him. But I didn't say any of it—not one word.

He started slowly for the tent.

In my mind it was as if time had slowed down, and that I was seeing a movie run one frame at a time.

I cleared my throat. ". . . Uh . . . I just . . . wanted to say . . ."

He stopped.

"Yeah?"

The seconds ticked by.

"I like it up here . . . in the wilderness."

He looked closely at me. "Yeah?"

"Yeah, it's so . . . basic. What would you think? . . . That is, can we do this again sometime, maybe in a few weeks, just the two of us?"

His Adam's apple moved laboriously as he swallowed. "You want to come up here again . . . with me?"

I nodded. "Yeah, well . . . we already got the back-packs. Might as well use 'em."

"Sure . . . might as well."

We could hear Jill in the tent break down, her sobs coming like huge gulps of emotion spilling out.

We listened to her crying.

"Women," Dad said, wiping his face with a sleeve.

"I know—they're such bawl babies," I said, turning so he wouldn't see my face.

Jill ran from the tent, barefoot, wearing a pair of Dad's long johns for pajamas, crazily hopping because of the rocks. She threw her arms around me and kissed me hard on the cheek, then rushed to Dad to hug and kiss him, then as quickly hopped back to the tent and into her sleeping bag.

"When do you want to go?" he asked, wiping his eyes.

"How about the fourth week in August?"

He nodded his head. "Sounds good. I think I'd like to try Misty Moon Lake. Of course, you don't get there from here."

"No?"

"Oh no—you go further on the highway out of Buf-falo before you turn off. Nice thing about Misty Moon is it's not that far to hike. And I'll tell you one thing—at

Misty Moon when they're taking lures, it's out of this world. There's a spinner called a Panther Martin. They say it sends sonar waves that drive fish crazy. At Misty Moon one time I had five strikes on one cast with a Panther Martin. And late August, when it cools down, it oughta be real good."

By morning the clouds had gone. Jill and I cooked breakfast. Dad got dressed and, before anything else, walked down to the lake. The bobber was floating motionless in the water.

"It came off," Dad said. "During the night. The fish'll be all right now."

"Sure," I agreed. "It'll be okay."

We stayed longer than we'd planned. Actually it was my idea.

It's strange how you can get used to anything. The first day we washed the pans with soap and boiling water. The second day I just walked out to the lake and swished the pan through the water a couple of times to let the bigger chunks fall off.

The third day, after we came back from fishing, Jill asked me to make her a cup of hot chocolate. I took the billy can and poured some hot water in her cup, but I was too tired to go hunting through our backpacks for a spoon. "Let's see," I said, looking on the ground, "what we need right now is a sterile stick. Aha, there's one." I picked up a stick and stirred the hot chocolate and gave it to her. She took it and drank without batting an eye.

On the fourth day I had to wash my jeans because they had fish blood all over them. After I'd borrowed a pair of Dad's jeans, I walked out to the lake, set my jeans in the water, put a stone on them, and came back to the camp.

"That's all you're gonna do?" Jill asked.

"I'll tell you how it works. I leave 'em in there overnight and just let the rotation of the earth swirl 'em clean."

The last evening there we ate up our food supply so we wouldn't have to carry it out. It was a banquet. We had strawberry Jell-O made by mixing the hot water and gelatin in a Zip-lock bag, then laying it in the lake. We made biscuits by wrapping Bisquick around a stick and heating it above hot coals. And we had macaroni and cheese and fish. For dessert Dad had a surprise. We took snow that still lay in occasional patches and mixed fruit punch mix with it. It tasted better than any snowcone you can buy.

We sat by the fire again and watched the patterns of light changing on the mountain peaks surrounding us.

The next day we packed and started down the trail.

"Daddy," Jill said, "after you and Jimmy go camping again, Scott and I want you to stay with us for a while."

"Yeah," I laughed. "Spoil their kids rotten."

"How about if I teach 'em how to fish?" he said.

"They'd love that," she said.

"And then after that, come down to California. I'll see if I can have you meet Ed McMahon or Doc."

"I don't care about that," he said. "I just want to meet Amy and your kid Provo."

I cleared my throat. Jill was smiling. "It's Logan, Dad."

"Logan, Provo, whatever."

We kept walking.

"Wonder when the *National Inquirer* will come out with the article about you," Dad said.

"You might even be on the cover," Jill teased.

"Hey, Jillsy, you think I'd make a good cover boy?"

She laughed, pausing on the trail to look at my crazy pose. The sweat beading up on her face was beginning to streak the protective layer of grime we'd all built up during our stay.

"Why not?" Dad said, so much more relaxed than when we first met him. "E.T. made it on a magazine cover. Jimmy looks at least that good."

Jill hooted. "All right! Way to go, Daddy!"

"Think you'd ever use that on Johnny Carson?" he asked me.

"Maybe so, Dad."

He smiled proudly. "How about that!"

We continued down the trail. I stumbled on a rock and nearly fell the rest of the way down the mountain. The backpack was rubbing on my sunburn. A swarm of mosquitoes was dogging me down the trail, treating my skin like a Whitman sampler.

My feet were killing me. Each rock on the trail dug at me through my now worn-out tennis shoes. I vowed if we ever got back to civilization I'd buy the best pair of boots they make, something that will last a few years.

For as long as my dad wants to lead me into the wilderness at Misty Moon.